I heard the chafing and then clacking noise of a pistol slide, reached the door, spotted an athletic man with bald spot and thin beard in a pale suit aiming at another man on a chair. He turned back to me with eyes widened in surprise. He merely had to pull the trigger and our mission would have failed.

My name is Monique Arnaud. I am a Mamba. My teammates and I were biochemically enhanced and trained by the Cartel as professional assassins. Now we're working for the Dragon empress as secret agents instead. Our mission is to extract the Cartel's instruments—Dragon technology experts—from their captivity.

The world-wide crime cartel is shattered, but still numerous graduates of the old Dragon technology university are in the hands of merciless criminals. To free them and win them as supporters for Johanna's defense efforts is the perfect challenge for her special unit, the Mambas. But such a mission bears high risk and doesn't always run smoothly. What kind of sacrifices must the fighters make to reach their goals?

Assassin
Copyright © 2021 Valerie J. Long
ISBN: 978-1-4874-2645-3
Cover art by Martine Jardin

Published by eXtasy Books Inc or
Devine Destinies, an imprint of eXtasy Books Inc

Look for us online at:
www.eXtasybooks.com or www.devinedestinies.com

ASSASSIN
ZOE LIONHEART BOOK 23
LIONESS TRACKS III

BY

VALERIE J. LONG

Chapter One: Aria Di Bravura

The approximately two-meter-high quarry wall meant no obstacle to me, although the dense moss growth had soaked up the morning dew and thus had become very slippery. The old trees on this side of the estate blocked every sight of the mansion — and vice versa. So I could simply jump up to the capstone and down the inner side again.

I looked to the right. Elodie had just let herself drop from a strong branch and showed me a circle of thumb and index finger — *all okay*. I returned the signal and glanced around once more.

If Sabine hadn't missed something, there were no electronic security measures in the park, no motion sensors, tripwires, or infrared light barriers — all the nice things Jo liked to talk about. Nevertheless, I checked again myself. Tess had instructed us at least a dozen times that we wouldn't become a disgrace to Jo — needlessly, as we all agreed on that. No noise, no shoot-out, silently in and out. Velvet-like, so to speak. The guards shouldn't even notice our visit.

I sneaked on and peered around the next tree. From here, I could observe the largest part of the terrace running all around the mansion's upper floor. Only few spots remained obstructed from my view by large bushes. Once Elodie had reached her position, she'd fill that gap.

I counted two guards on this side of the house, both armed with short-barreled machine pistols. That matched Sabine's reconnaissance mission results — two guards on the terrace at each of the mansion's four sides, and two again at the main

1

entrance on the ground level. The two on our side didn't appear very alert—not as if they'd seriously expect uninvited visitors.

Tess had said that probably nobody expected a second retrieval wave. Back then, when we had freed the reluctant and destructive instruments, we had faced substantial resistance after the first simple pickups. Presumably, back then they had been alarmed here, too. But that lay two years in the past.

A bird's chirp sounded from the right—Elodie had reached her position.

Just at this moment, the guard to the left raised a hand to his ear, and the other looked up and peered in Elodie's direction. Next, shots sounded from the left side—from the main entrance, where Tess and Sabine would approach.

CHAPTER TWO

I heard not only the rattling of several machine pistols, but also the hiss of plasma rounds. Sabine hadn't mentioned that!

Our secondary goal of a *quiet* mission had therefore failed, and put our primary target in imminent lethal danger — if the guard staff was still following their order of instantly killing the *instrument* in case of a liberation attempt.

I signaled a Three to Elodie. *Opponent's strength unknown, fight inevitable — strike firmly, eliminate identified targets as reliably as possible.*

She answered with three raised fingers — acknowledgement.

Good.

Upon dashing forward I checked for options to reach the upper terrace through the greens. Through under that bush, jump up the gray brick wall, grab the ledge, and swing over the stone railing — okay.

The guard noticed me as soon as I came out under the trees and swung his machine pistol around. Too late!

He had three seconds overall while I had to cover the hundred meters to the house and up to his place, and on the last third of my way, the bushes obstructed his sight. Too short to stop a *fast* determined Mamba.

He just had time for a surprised shout but didn't manage to fire his gun — with the drive that carried me over the balustrade, my kick met his chin hard enough to make his cervical spine give in. Before I landed, he was already dead.

Elodie's opponent shared this fate.

A quick glance constituted our agreement. Plan Three — enter the building, search for primary target.

The trellised door almost in front of me stood open. I jumped through and rolled away to come to a halt ready for a jump.

No guard in this room, so I hurried to the door, opened it a bit and listened. Aside from the outside shots' echo I heard quickly tapping steps. More guards? If so, they were on their way to the entrance as reinforcements, or to their *host* as executioners.

I sensed Elodie behind me and quickly pulled the door open.

Three more armed men were just running down the large open stairs to our right — led by a blond giant with a bulky plasma rifle, followed by a bald-headed man with large-caliber pistol and a dark-curly-haired youngster with machine pistol. Without hesitation, I jumped over the balcony railing between the leading two men.

First I had to batter bald-head's guns aside and make the giant lose his balance with a kick. Oops — the kick caused less effect than hoped for, and the giant only stumbled a few steps down, just enough extra distance to get his gun barrel up. I couldn't take care of that, though, because bald-head was about to throw himself upon me with a loud roar — well, I ducked down deep, slipped through under his arms, then pushed myself up and catapulted him behind me, right into the giant.

Before I tended to those two again, I saw Elodie crush the youngster's windpipe with little remorse. *Three.* No opponents at our backs, no witnesses.

CHAPTER THREE

The giant tossed bald-head aside and drew a knife. With it, he was surely more agile than with his rifle, but that wouldn't help him. I immediately attacked him again.

My next kick didn't take him off-balance again. Instead, he grabbed my foot with one hand and stabbed my upper leg with his knife. But the blade didn't pierce my thin nano armor's robust fabric.

Thanks, Jo.

Sadly, I was still stuck with him while bald-head aimed his pistol in my direction. Elodie took care of the latter problem for me—she jumped down the stairs, kicked the gun aside, and then hit bald-head's nose from below.

My blond giant was already dead, too, he just didn't know it yet. He tried another stab, this time at my face. Without letting my foot go, he couldn't get close enough, though. Evading him was no effort. Instead, I took the hilt with my gloved right hand, jumped up, pulled myself forward at his knife hand, and kicked his face with force.

He deserved respect for still not letting me go. I had to live with a painful backward drop on the stairs—*ouch*—but now I could place my free foot on his chest, pull at his knife hand and lift him into the air.

He'd probably have put such a maneuver past a dainty girl like me. He didn't find time for further contemplation, as Elodie grabbed his head and turned it with a jerk. The cervical bones gave in, and the giant collapsed.

We briefly glanced at each other. From the upper floor

came the sound of splintering glass, so another team was about to intrude the house there. There was still shooting outside the main entrance.

It seemed we were the first. I pointed to the left of the open stairs, and Elodie nodded. So I hurried to the right.

One door behind the stairs stood ajar. Dim light simmered through, and I spotted some steps. The way to the cellar?

If our target was there, and *if* the half-open door meant it wasn't alone there, there might only be seconds left to fulfill the mission objective. *Fast.* I tore the door open and made one long leap down the stairs.

Light shone from another half-open door in the damp and dusty cellar corridor.

I heard the chafing and then clacking noise of a pistol slide, reached the door, spotted an athletic man with bald spot and thin beard in a pale suit aiming at another man on a chair. He turned back to me with eyes widened in surprise.

He merely had to pull the trigger and our mission would have failed. Unthinkable! My legs catapulted me forward *fast* — in flight I batted the pistol aside, kicked the shooter's head, and then landed at the far side of the room.

One brief look around sufficed. The room was secured.

I rose and straightened and addressed the man on the chair. "Mr. Salim Hadid?"

"Who are you?" He shook his head. "*What* are you? That was inhumanly fast!"

I didn't want to comment on his second question and his remark. "I'm Monique, and I've come to free you."

"Ha! Free me? Once I step outside, I'm pretty much dead."

I poked my last victim with my foot. "As dead as this one?"

Salim cocked his head. "Right — how did you get in here? What about the other guards?"

"Dead. In any case, until we're upstairs again."

He frowned. "Once again — what are you? A paid killer?"

I shrugged. "I'm compensated for killing your kidnappers and prison guards, so this label applies. Right now I'm your bodyguard — if you want."

"If I want. So I have a choice?"

"Of course. You can simply leave. Upstairs there's nobody left to stop you."

"Why are you doing this, then?"

"Because I believe in doing the right thing for mankind."

"The right thing for mankind — by killing kidnappers?"

"No. By freeing experts who can help the people in their fight against Jellies — if they want to."

He remained silent for a while. "Now tell me what's going on here."

I smiled at him. "The Legata Aurea, Johanna Meier, doubtlessly known to you as the Meier effect inventor, sent out her guard to free as many Dragon technology experts as possible. If you like, she may find good use for you at her new Dragon technology university."

CHAPTER FOUR

"Johanna Meier is dead," he said, after getting over his initial surprise.

"She feigned her death for the Cartel. Whatever you've heard—she's alive."

"Johanna's alive." He placed his hands together, leaned forward in his chair and looked down. "And the Cartel?"

"Decapitated and wrecked. Her doing."

"Johanna? Impossible."

Elodie appeared in the door. "The word *impossible* doesn't exist in great leaders' dictionaries. I think that quote comes from our Sheik's grandfather."

Salim looked up. "Another? How many are you?"

"Six," my partner replied. "Sufficient for this mission. It's all clear upstairs. If you like, we can leave. Tess said, we shouldn't wait for some hidden time fuse to trigger because there's nobody left to hit the dead-man switch."

"Oh." Salim rose. "So I must make up my mind now?"

"You should come with us for now. If you like, we can take you to the island, and if you don't want to stay, you can still leave. Jo said, though, once you've seen what we've accomplished, you won't want to leave."

He sighed. "Knowledge alone won't do, no matter how ingenious she is. Without nano technology we'll need centuries to reach the same level as before the destruction of Frostdragon. How often did I tell my jailers? That can't be conjured up from nothing, no matter how many experts you kidnap."

"Have a close look at our suits."

He shrugged. "Very figure-hugging, so what?"

"Those are light nano armors from current production."

"*What?*"

He reached for my arm, felt the surface, tried to see details in the dim light, then he looked up into my face. "Take me to your island."

CHAPTER FIVE

Tess rose and stepped into our plane's center aisle. She gave our sleeping protégé a side glance. His energy had lasted to give him some excitement upon sight of the aircraft, but soon after take-off he had fallen asleep and was now dozing away.

"Gals, that was sloppy work. We achieved the primary goal, okay, but at what cost? Eighteen dead! Not that I'd shed a tear for any of them, but if that goes public, Jo will face real heat. *Dragon empress sends out killer team* — that can't be."

"There are no witnesses," her partner Sabine argued.

"Of course there's a witness," Tess corrected. "The one who we couldn't eliminate. And now imagine if we'd found further prisoners, or unarmed playgirls, or a few domestics."

"We weren't prepared for that," Justine noted.

"No, we weren't. We have no rules of engagement for this case — a severe shortfall." Tess examined us all. "That's my responsibility. Jo trusted the mission lead to me. I won't blame any of you, but I urge you to help me so I don't miss anything else. For example — did we leave traces?"

"No, I don't think so," Sabine said. "Or?"

"The bodies." Tia rose. "The cause of death is clear — broken neck or suffocation from a crushed windpipe or a blunt skull trauma, and so on. That won't pose any pathologist a riddle. The riddle is — how could an unknown number of unarmed intruders kill so many armed, experienced guards without getting hurt themselves. At least none of us left traces of own blood, despite the many shots."

Tess nodded. "Correct. We should consider that, too. How can we avoid that in the future—aside from the fact that we shouldn't get into such a situation? But back to the traces we left. What else?"

"Footprints in the area," I chimed in. "Soil we carried into the house under our soles. A broken window."

Justine cocked her head. "We had to be quick."

"No accusation." Tess nodded at me. "More?"

Tia's observation still bothered me. "I can only speak for our side—but except at the front of the mansion the guards didn't get to shoot, right? That means our footprints will be found, inside as well as outside, and someone will ask why the guards didn't shoot."

"In the garden one could guess they were distracted by the shooting at the front," Elodie added. "But inside, on the open stairs, they'd have stood a good chance—against ordinary opponents."

"Could you tell that?" Tess asked. "That they stood a good chance, I mean."

"Yes, sure," Elodie replied. "When we came in, they were halfway down the stairs. They had all the time in the world."

Tess's question was aimed another way, I recognized. So I foresaw her next question. "Right. That'd be conspicuous, given you knew when the three came down the stairs in the course of the shooting. What if we'd already been at the foot of the stairs, hiding there? No, I think the evidence allows that conclusion."

Elodie frowned, but then nodded. "Yes, that's plausible."

Sabine raised her hand and spoke up when Tess nodded at her. "This would also explain why the intruders didn't use guns. Only if you don't make any noise can you get so deep inside the house and take the guards on the stairs by surprise. So it appears as if the attackers hadn't used guns because they wanted to be quiet, and not because they are so good—or at least not just because of that."

"Okay." Tess nodded. "That means nobody can automatically infer our involvement, more so as our *handwriting* isn't known yet. That must remain so—we must not be predictable, neither in advance nor afterward."

Chapter Six: Aria Cantabile

If I hadn't known it was in fact a prison, I could have appreciated the villa's ceiling-to-floor glass front. The view from the terrace over the beach and bay had to be marvelous, and if you wouldn't — or weren't allowed to — take a swim in the ocean, the huge pool offered a good alternative.

The little details spoiled the impression. Firstly, there was the double two-meter-high chain-link fence surrounding the estate. The outer fence was crowned by barbed wire, the inner one was charged, as the little red light-emitting diodes told us. There was the allegedly relaxed guy in his pale Hawaiian shirt who didn't know better than to linger on the terrace for hours and gaze out to the sea and beach. There was the young man who had made himself comfortable on the coconut mat on the beach before the small gate. He had a beautiful sixpack, very small swimmers, *oh là là,* and with his black tousled hair he embodied the perfect Latin lover. Only — what did he do here besides watching the passersby on the beach?

If he wasn't castrated or differently interested, his self-control was admirable. He didn't even turn his head in our direction when Elodie and I, only wearing tiny thongs, approached along the water line. Where Elodie's boobs were doubtlessly as much worth a glance as mine.

Of course, we couldn't see what was going on behind his mirrored sunglasses, just as he couldn't see what we were looking at behind our sunglasses. But we had both turned our heads toward him, and we also admired the villa — so much so that we now stopped.

I raised one hand and pointed at the wooden panels that shielded a part of the terrace against gazes and wind. "Look," I said toward Elodie, "that must be a gigantic pool up there."

"I bet you'd swim in the nude up there," my partner replied. "And after, you can sit down in the sun for drying with a glass of champagne."

"For drying?"

"Well, yes — I wouldn't object to a hot pool boy ensuring at least *one* spot remains nicely wet." She leant toward me and whispered, "Like this one here."

Her words were loud enough that he could hear us anyway. Without taking my gaze away from his crotch, I answered at the same volume, "I'd rather have a larger one."

"He only needs a versatile tongue."

"Nah, at least I'd like to see his excitement. I won't admit wet noodles to my pussy."

"And what about me?"

"That doesn't count — you have no dick."

The young man didn't react to our naughty remarks. I got the impression that his swimmers fit a bit tighter, but otherwise he remained the ice-cold security pro. In his role as neutral beach guest, he failed epically though.

Instead, the guard on the terrace didn't merely show professional interest. He rested both arms on the railing, and with a smile he watched the two scarcely-clad women who invested so much effort into his colleague on the sand. Doubtlessly, that would be the cue for some banter after duty — unless they had other worries to discuss by then.

In any case, Elodie and I had accomplished the first part of our mission and distracted both guards on this side. Before we lost credibility in our own role, I placed one arm around my partner's hip and pulled her along.

I didn't doubt the two guards' gazes followed our

uncovered, rhythmically swaying backsides for a long while. This should give Tess and Sabine more than enough time to enter the premises.

Chapter Seven

After our slow stroll, Elodie and I reached a livelier beach section. Here, we could be sure about receiving everything from benevolent-interested to lecherous-voyeuristic male glances. We weren't by far the only topless women, and also not the only ones in good shape, but we had two decisive advantages—firstly, we were confident about our good looks. After all, we were training hard. Secondly, we had systematically been trained for nude appearances, so we were used to acting cool even in the presence of the greatest lewd assholes—any Mamba candidates who had failed in this subject were dead. To know that none of the men on this beach wanted to kill us was a tremendously relaxing thought, so we could stay easy—and that worked to our advantage.

The only important aspect was that people remembered our tits and asses and not our sunglasses-covered faces.

Doubtlessly, the disappointment was huge when we reached our bag parked in the sand and covered ourselves with tops and shorts. One or another sporty guy might even have appealed to me—but for one, those guys were already in company, and for two, we still had a mission to accomplish.

Our robust all-terrain car without roof or doors was parked not far from the beach. Elodie just tossed our bag inside before slipping behind the wheel.

I mounted the second seat and grinned at her. "Giddy up."

She smiled and activated the power supply, tossed a routine glance at the mirror, and drove off. With a silent hum, we rolled toward the main street and followed it out of town.

A little later, Elodie turned into a small access road. She stopped when the already familiar house with the large glass panes came into sight. A small sign at the roadside declared the rest of the road private property.

"Have a look at the map," Elodie told me — or potential listeners and lip readers.

I nodded and fetched a paper map — a concession to this remote area, where a handheld computer wouldn't always have reception. At the same time, it was the perfect tool for us to hide from the guards' eyes.

The plan granted us three minutes to find the right way on the map. Three minutes for Tess and Sabine to get their protégé out.

Three minutes to find out if this mission would remain silent or result in a big shootout — in which case we'd have to find cover quickly. Protective suits didn't match our role, so the two of us weren't wearing any. We knowingly accepted that risk.

After all, we were *Mambas. Even naked more deadly than a soldier company*, that was our motto. Protective suits were a nice add-on, but not a mandatory part of our equipment.

Three hundred meters was way out of range for pistols and machine pistols, and at least a challenge for a rifle shooter. At the same time, it was a long distance for Tess and Sabine and their *instrument.*

"Something's stirring," Elodie reported.

I moved my head to be able to see something through my little hole in the map. Indeed — covered by the scraggy bushes, three people in sand-colored camouflage suits were sneaking up toward us. The single guard on this side of the building was still only watching us.

The approaching other team needed a distraction now. My cue!

I jumped out of the car, grabbed a tissue box from the rear

seat, and hurried between the bushes to relieve myself there — at least it should look like that to the guard. After all, he shouldn't watch anything but my bare butt for a short time.

Meanwhile, Elodie tried to turn the car around on the narrow piece of road, the driver's side facing the house. Her awkward performance, turning the wheel while stopping, should allow our teammates and their protégé to climb into the car unseen.

Elodie finishing her turn was the sign for me our people were aboard. I pulled up my pants, hurried back to the car, tossed the tissue box onto the floor and jumped into my seat.

Elodie firmly pushed the pedal. The car leaped forward spraying small pebbles away. With matching verve, she turned onto the main road.

I glanced into the back. "Problems?"

"No," Tess replied. "Everything went as planned."

"Are we safe now?" a soft voice chimed in.

"Stay low," Sabine answered. She was covering the rescued Dragon technology graduate with her body. "The criminals have connections to the local police. It's over once we're out of here. Don't worry, we've got all that covered."

Elodie was already steering the car to the curb. A station wagon with tinted windows was waiting there. "You can change cars now."

Tess stepped outside first to have a look around. "Clear. Come."

Sabine rose, let her protégé sit up, and nodded at me. "Good luck."

"Same to you. Have a good flight."

Elodie waited until the station wagon had left, then she followed to the next intersection, where our ways parted. Tess and Sabine would take the researcher to our Tigershark and thus take her safely — and invisibly — out of the country.

We'd end our vacation like two ordinary tourists. No one

should make a connection between us and the researcher's sudden disappearance. A concurrent departure would only be suspicious.

CHAPTER EIGHT

We acted appropriately surprised when two policemen intercepted us half an hour later upon arrival at our hotel.

"Be quiet and come along," was the only comment that the more talkative one offered. He pushed me hard onto the police car's back seat, slammed the door shut, and then entered the front.

Elodie and I glanced at each other, and she shrugged and frowned. But she didn't speak, as we had been instructed. Every travel guide advised in grave words how to deal with the police in this country, that is, submissively. Defiant, sassy, or otherwise insubordinate people soon found themselves in penal camps, lawfully sentenced for civil disorder or misconduct toward a police officer. Only high-ranking politicians could afford to protest against such treatment. Nevertheless, the country was a popular vacation destination, because as long as one didn't cross the police, it was regarded as very safe — even and especially for pretty young women.

With regard to our role, we principally had nothing to fear.

They led me — of course separated from Elodie — to a small office and let me sit down on a plain wooden chair. Two policemen stood watch to both sides of the door while I was staring past the desk with its piles of files through the dusty window.

The two uniformed men left the room when an athletic mid-fiftyish man in a pale summer suit entered. His

aftershave smelled expensive and intrusive. He didn't intro-
duce himself, only placed his jacket over the backrest of his
own, clearly more comfortable seat, and dropped onto that
seat.

"Name?" he snapped.

"Monique Arnaud."

"So." He briefly examined my face, then he fetched a file
from one of his piles and pretended to find something about
me in it. "France?"

"Belgium."

"So. I didn't think anyone would still live there."

"It's okay around Brussels," I quietly commented, trying
not to sound defiant. It was possible that he was really trying
to make nice conversation. Even if he was corrupt, he didn't
have to be a mean guy.

"What are you doing there? What's your job?"

There he touched the most difficult part of our cover stories. It could neither be a job in politics, nor a dubious occu-
pation which would trigger ideas for mistreating us. "Courier
services."

"What kind of stuff?"

"All kind of urgent documents — we must not look inside."

He smiled. "But sometimes you do it anyway?"

"No, of course not. I check whether the envelopes are
properly sealed upon pickup."

"Okay." He closed his file and let it slap on the table. "Why
are you here?"

"Pardon?" I shrugged and gazed at him. "I don't know."

"Don't play games with me. You were interested in a villa
today."

"Oh, that — yes, I liked that house. Right at the beach.
We've been there a second time, I guess — when we tried to
find another beach access to pick up our sun-frocks."

"Don't tell me bullshit."

"No, surely not. Well, we took a boat to the beach end to walk back along the shoreline from there. But then Elodie said she wouldn't want to carry the frock, and we could pick it up later. So we left the sun-frocks there and started our walk without."

"Without sun-frocks."

"Yes. After all, we still had our other stuff at our spot — that is, these shorts and the top."

"You simply left it there?"

"This is a very safe country, I've read." I showed him a cautious smile.

"What were you looking for at the access road to the villa?"

"The beach access. We took an early turn." I hesitated. "Oh, and then I had to take a leak."

"So." He rose and came around his desk to plant himself before me. It should look intimidating, so I shrank in my seat and gave him a frightened look.

"You're not aware of your situation."

"N-n-no?"

"This is, as you read correctly, a very safe country. It's safe here because we make sure nobody walks all over the police. Nobody pulls our legs. We expect unconditional respect, you know?"

"Yes."

"I don't think so. You know, if someone's disrespectful to me, it takes one phone call and we have a date with the judge. Disrespect — the judge calls it misdemeanor toward officials — is punished severely. Depending on the case, the sentence can be up to four weeks in educational camp. You know why it's called like that?"

"N-n-no?"

"You will be educated about respect. Whatever happens there, you will respect your teachers. Once you're there, no judge will decide on punishments. The teachers may do everything necessary to gain respect. *Everything,* you understand?"

I understood quite well, but according to my role, I couldn't know he was talking about beatings and rape by the teachers. However, I didn't have to know it.

"Please — I'm respecting you very much!"

He leaned down to me. At this distance, his aftershave could no longer hide his smell of alcohol. "So tell me the truth now. Get it out!"

He couldn't know that he couldn't threaten me. During our training in the ZONE we had learned everything about this kind of respect. *Everything* — and in contrast to that, the educated weren't slowly strangled to death in this country. Such a camp wouldn't be more than a rough adventure vacation to me.

"I'm telling the truth already," I replied in a trembling voice. "We're just on a beach vacation. Please. I'll be very respectful." Saying that, I opened my knees with hesitation.

The quickie I thus offered him was a minor sacrifice that I gladly gave for the mission — for Johanna — even though she didn't know anything about it. She — as *Velvet* — had shown us what respect really meant. We had been trained to kill, had been told our next target was Velvet. She had come, had freed us from our trainers' grip, had relieved us from our drug addiction, and then had given us the choice to follow her or go our own way. I'd give my life for this woman, and I was sure all my sisters-in-arms fared the same.

"We will see," my interrogator said, straightened himself before me, and opened his fly.

Accepting my fate, I leaned forward and grabbed his fast-growing cock.

"No." He took my chin and pulled me up. "Turn around and drop your pants."

So I did that, and patiently waited until he had come inside me.

Next, he packed his tool away, walked to the door, and called his colleagues in. "Take her downstairs."

CHAPTER NINE

You couldn't expect much comfort from a wooden pallet in a dark and sticky basement cell. I took it as a good sign that they hadn't provided me with a bucket—if that wasn't meant to literally put me under pressure, my stay wouldn't be long. One hour in such a hole, where the only light came from a row of dim yellow LEDs shining through the palm-sized door window, should suffice to wear the average prisoner down.

"No chats," the young policeman had harshly advised me and then pushed me into my cell with one hand on my buttocks.

They couldn't do much worse as long as they had to consider my innocence—unless they'd just make up some civil disorder.

Someone sneezed in the adjacent cell.

I sneezed back and cleared my throat, and got another harrumph as reply.

Good—Elodie was next door and unhurt. So we'd wait.

Aside from our smooth breathing, the only noise was a distant, cadenced dripping. It might have been meant to make the ambience appear even more dismal, but it offered us an opportunity to estimate the passage of time.

First, I had to determine the interval between two drops. Thereafter, I could derive the number of drops per minute and begin the actual counting. Until then, five or six minutes had already passed, but that didn't matter.

It really wasn't easy to focus on counting for such a long time and keep the thoughts from going astray, but we had learned numerous meditation techniques during our Mamba training so that we could keep control of ourselves. This had been crucial for survival, too — those who lost it under the accelerator drugs' permanent influence were eliminated.

Elodie was collected after eighty-eight or eighty-nine minutes. She bade farewell with two short sniffs.

I continued counting. Another quarter of an hour later, it was my turn. The cell door opened, and a policeman barked, "Come on out."

Obedient and with my gaze on the floor I followed him. *Oh yes, we have learned the hard way to play the submissive!*

I very much hoped I wouldn't have to show them the other side. But if only one of the policemen saw past our disguise or recognized our special abilities, we'd have to cover our traces. Ultimately.

"There you are again," my interrogator welcomed me. "Sit down."

He waited until I had taken my seat. Then he tried to pierce me with his stare. I let my gaze wander back and forth, across his desk, to the window, to the walls, rubbed my hands at the chair's edge and inhaled in short breaths.

"Well. What can you tell me?"

His question led to the crucial point of our cover story. Whatever I told him had to match Elodie's statement — but not precise enough to appear concerted or learned by heart. I couldn't afford to fail.

"There was another car," I began and waited for his reaction.

He only nodded.

"Briefly, after we left the access road." I licked my upper lip. "Tinted windows. I only thought how square that looks — but now, the place strikes me odd. That wasn't the place to have a break."

"Do you know the license number? Or the make?"

I squinted. "No. An antenna stub on the roof. Dark green. And a long scratch at the left side. I thought that's ugly. But I don't remember the brand."

He reclined in his chair with a sigh. "If you remember, will you call me?"

"Oh — yes, sure, of course!"

Of course not. Nobody would voluntarily return into the police's grasp after such a visit — you'd rather remain thoroughly intoxicated for the rest of your stay than remembering anything — I could see he knew that, too.

But he had played his hand, and this was everything he'd gained. He knew it — he wasn't to get any more from us. He had no reasonable grounds for suspecting. We had simply been in the wrong place at the wrong time. In turn, he had a lead — an unknown car with a remarkable scratch. He just couldn't take too much time, or this track would be cold.

Two young women were just a distraction. The little fun we could offer — and would offer him if he'd only release us — couldn't compensate for the trouble the criminals would cause him if he didn't work for his bribes.

"You may go," he finally said.

CHAPTER TEN

Elodie was waiting for me outside the precinct door. "I had hoped they'd let you go, too," she explained for potential eavesdroppers. "Shall we go?"

"Seems we have to. Or should we take a taxi?"

"I could do with a little exercise now."

"Well then."

So we went on foot.

A few blocks on, Elodie pointed at a café. "How about that?"

"We have to leave," I said.

"It went well, didn't it?"

"Too well. We're no longer safe."

"Why do you say that?"

"The chit on his desk with our room number. I can't prove it, but I'm sure our next hosts won't be so kind to us."

"What are you thinking of?"

"The kidnappers. They'll have questions — and they won't be considerate. Our lives won't count."

"So?"

"Abort."

She glanced around. "Which way?"

"I'd prefer a silent solution."

"Naturally. We shouldn't get close to the hotel anymore. They'll be waiting for us there for sure." She squinted. "But they won't bet on it."

I followed her gaze and saw the two young bullies who were approaching us. "Looks like a little game. Only — how should we proceed?"

Elodie smiled. "It's too obvious. Should we find out what they've prepared for us?"

"No."

"Okay. In that case, let's take the road over there."

"Fine."

We dashed away, without boost, but still at a speed the two bullies couldn't match.

They didn't have to match us, I recognized three hundred meters later. There, two other guys were already waiting for us, and these two drew their guns once they saw us running.

Twenty more meters to cover — no problem!

I whistled and *accelerated.*

Elodie did the same.

Ah!

The men before us had no chance — before they could level their guns, they were unconscious, and now *we* had their guns.

That was the last our pursuers saw of us. They preferred to find cover, and we disappeared around the next corner. Another short sprint took us to a small shopping center's parking lot.

Whoops.

The older gentleman just managed to stop his convertible when we turned into the access lane before him. His passenger stared at us wide-eyed — oh, yes, the guns.

I smiled at her, walked four steps along the car and swung onto the seat behind her. Elodie took the seat behind the driver.

"Drive on," I sharply commanded. "Don't look back."

The driver obeyed. He had seen the guns, too.

I wasn't in the mood to tell him that we wouldn't hurt them. I still felt the booster's rush. Even if the addictive component was missing — being *fast* turned me on. The wetness in my crotch soaked my shorts.

Elodie smelled the same, and she was slightly trembling. We had to calm down soon.

"Take us to the animal park," I ordered. There we could vanish in the crowd or change dress in the souvenir shop.

"What are you going to do with us?" the driver dared to ask. His passenger nudged him, but didn't speak up herself.

"Nothing. Just drive."

CHAPTER ELEVEN

When we reached the animal park access, I said, "Stop." The car stopped, and I pushed myself up to sit on its beltline. "I beg your pardon for the shock, and for not being able to offer you compensation. I can only give you a little advice — it's better for you if you can't remember. The police interrogation cells are uncomfortable."

I swung my legs outside, slipped down to the road and walked toward the park entrance. A few meters on I found a trash container to drop my gun into.

Elodie followed me. She still trembled slightly.

"So bad?" I asked.

"Y-y-yes. It dissipates slowly."

"Come." I led her to the restrooms and there into the spacious disabled stall. It was quiet in the early afternoon — there were no new arrivals anymore, and no visitors taking a break before departure yet.

The simplest way to dissipate the booster and calm the adrenalized mind was an orgasm. So I closed the door behind us, wrapped my arms around Elodie, and kissed her.

Her tongue answered with enthusiasm. She unbuttoned her shorts, then mine, plucked the bows of her and my thong, and next, her trembling fingers were between my slippery wet lips.

My right hand clawed into her buttocks while I began to rub her right nipple with my left hand. At the same time, I lifted my right leg, so that she could rub her crotch against it.

No.

That wouldn't do. She needed her climax more urgently than I. So I took my left hand down and began to massage her crotch. It didn't take her long to come with a loud moan.

I felt hot, wet, unsatisfied — but I only hugged my teammate tight.

Elodie took a few deep breaths, and then she pushed me away. "Thank you."

Instead of answering, I briefly shook her hand.

Then I pulled up my shorts and stuffed the thong into my pocket. "To the ferry?"

"To the ferry." She hesitated, then she shrugged and put on her shorts, too. "Straight to the port?"

"Let's buy some souvenirs first."

Elodie looked cute in her blue summer dress with the big white plush parrot on her arm. The way she balanced on her sky-blue stiletto heels, swaying her butt, countless male gazes followed her on her way to the ferry terminal.

I didn't look ugly either in my thin, wide-cut white linen pants, the ocean-blue canvas sneakers, and the rosy balloon top, but drew significantly less attention. That way I could watch for men who might be after us.

Perhaps the small gang that had kept our instrument captive wasn't that well organized, or perhaps they didn't expect us to leave that soon and by ferry — in any case, nobody prevented us from boarding the ship.

Together with many other guests, Elodie headed to one of the bars aboard, and I followed her with a little distance.

She smiled at a single young man who was visibly happy about her interest — he invited her for a glass of sparkling wine right away. They spent the next twenty minutes talking about trivia.

Once the ferry had sailed, I joined my teammate. "Hello, Elodie."

Then I reached out my hand to her benefactor. "I'm Monique."

"Toni." He shook my hand, but he looked disappointed. "Hello. I thought Elodie was alone."

I held his hand longer than necessary while she placed one hand on his shoulder.

"You know," she began quietly. "This will be a long passage. Such a journey can be lonesome and boring, or very entertaining and diverse."

"Well."

She leaned close to his ear, licked it, and whispered, "I'm sure you're strong enough for both of us. And if you need a break, you might want to watch us?"

"Well."

"She's a real lap cat," I added. "Or a wild tiger. But if you suck her earlobe, she'll do everything you want."

"Don't listen to Monique." Elodie stepped behind him and placed her hand on his leg. "She's got only one goal—she wants to drink your cum. She likes nothing more than sucking a hard rod while I'm keeping her pussy busy."

"You're pulling my leg."

"No, surely not, Toni." My mate's hand wandered inward. "There are very different things we want to do with you, and you'll never regret this passage."

And we'd disappear without trace for the rest of the journey. In any case, we couldn't be found in our own cabin.

CHAPTER TWELVE: ARIA AGITATA

With her big toe, Tia flicked a small heap of wet sand toward her partner Justine.

"Who is it this time?" she asked.

We were sitting on Velvet Island's beach together. After the daily fitness workout, our leader had summoned us to a mission briefing.

Tess shielded her eyes against the sun and glanced at the dossier in her hand.

"His name is Peter Berg. He's forty-six years old, Norwegian, and specialized in nano healing. He's held captive in a lodge in the Canadian Rockies. According to the logs, the Cartel had hoped to learn from him how to use nano technology to improve human fighting abilities. He only agreed to treat their people with injuries or radiation injuries. Only selected members were allowed to enjoy such a treatment, and even those only under strictest security measures—they didn't want the patients to learn about the location. Well, as usual, that data isn't up to date anymore."

"Who will explore?" Tia asked. "Sabine and you?"

Tess nodded. "Yes, we're going ahead, but we'll take you along as backup. Maybe we'll have to decide on immediate access while we're there."

She gazed at each of us in turn—her partner Sabine, Tia and Justine, Elodie and me, and finally Gwen and Avril.

"Four teams this time. The lodge is—or was—well guarded due to the visitor traffic. The Cartel deliberately chose bear territory to keep the guests from foolish actions, so the guards carry large-caliber guns. Due to the larger number of guards and due to the bears, our mission will be more difficult, and it's possible that we won't get a second chance. That's why I want to have the option to act right away—either in the unlikely case we're discovered or because the situation is simply favorable."

Tess waved to our pilot. "Zoé, that means we'll incorporate you and your Tigershark into our plans from the beginning, in case we'll have to quickly get away with Peter. Close, low, and disguised."

"No problem." Our *little lioness* remained relaxed. Even if the lodge turned out to be armed with anti-air missiles, she'd calmly come with her disguised Tigershark to pick us up and take us to safety.

"What about perimeter safety?" Gwen asked.

"One moment, Gwen. Before we get to planning, I'd like to address the rules of play." Tess waited for our nods. "Firstly—all patients we meet there have some kind of skeletons in their closets. They don't deserve tender treatment. Secondly—although female Cartel members were cured there, too, the staff is male-dominated, as usual. Peter has a small team of female assistants for his medical work, and he might want to take them along. Moreover, there will be entertainers for guests and staff—whatever they're doing there can hardly be held against them, right, gals?"

Some lowered their heads, some shook them, and Tia made a grim face, just like me. A young woman could only survive in such an environment by enduring unspeakable things, and sometimes even taking part in them. Other people might condemn such behavior, but we couldn't.

"Maybe we'll have to take the entertainers along, too, if they want to come. What I really want to say is this—we might come to the conclusion we'll have to clean up the entire location. This one might be more than a *quiet* thieving spree.

We'll equip our plasma pistols."

"Phat." Avril bent backward and stared up to the palms. "Can we fit all those people into the plane at once? How many assistants and entertainers are there?"

"Two and eight were the last count," Tess said. "Jo marked an internal note. According to it, the number was limited and the entertainers could only be replaced in exceptional cases. The Cartel didn't want their hideout to stand out due to a long series of missing girls. Therefore, certain sadistic practices are forbidden — lucky girls. Otherwise, Jo would have placed this target on top of the list."

"Eleven guests and eight of us," Zoé computed. "That'll be cramped — the Tigershark regularly offers space for twelve, and the co-pilot's seat is free."

"What if we remove a few seats?" Sabine asked. "I'd say, it doesn't have to do for the long distance."

"I'll check that," Zoé said.

"Slow down, gals," Tess intervened. "Fact check first. I'll hand out the dossiers now, and you read them all. Then we'll clarify question about the situation. Once we all have the same picture, we'll start planning. Discipline, please."

"Yes, mum," Justine replied, and it wasn't meant as irony. We all were still alive only because we had listened to Tess and had placed discipline first. We were successful because we stuck to tried and tested rules.

Most of all, it was unthinkable to disappoint Jo. Doing less than our best was out of the question, from the mission's first to its last minute. Effective now.

Chapter Thirteen

The small mountain creek hadn't looked so raging and deep on the aerial photos. Many of the rocks that should have offered a comfortable crossing according to our plan were now covered knee-deep in white foam.

Elodie frowned and looked around. I shook my head. We had no time for long detours, so this was the best place to cross.

I waved the signal for *jumping*. She nodded, aimed at a spot on the other side, and jumped. The humid ground over there gave in a bit, and her foot slipped a few centimeters down, but she compensated both with a bent knee, and came to a safe stand.

Five steps on, she reached the trees' cover. Her green-brown checkered camo suit and her camo paint blended in with the surroundings. She gazed and listened around.

All clear, she signaled.

I jumped after her and landed in the same spot. My foot slipped away, too. I bent a bit deeper, shifted my weight to the other leg and stabilized my position.

Elodie grinned.

Go on, I signaled and then followed my own advice.

At least we hadn't met the bear whose track we had crossed a few minutes before. The animal could hardly endanger us — we were too fast for that — but it could give us away.

Now came the time to focus on the task ahead of us — should Tess send the signal, we had to be able to react *instantly*, and until she did, no one should spot us.

If you could *be seen, assume you* will *be seen.*

Even our camouflage's protection was limited, so we couldn't enter the area visible from the lodge. In the undulating terrain, we therefore couldn't approach closer than three hundred meters.

Of course we still wanted to watch what was going on there. For this purpose, we used a periscope with pinhead-sized lenses. Across this distance, an observer inside the lodge wouldn't be able to tell it from a little bug.

The matching directional microphone wasn't any larger.

While I examined the image projected on my palm and listened to the recorded noises, Elodie kept an eye on our surroundings. As long as everything went according to Tess's desires, this wouldn't change for a long time.

CHAPTER FOURTEEN

If you could *be heard, assume you* will *be heard.* If necessary, Elodie and I communicated by gesture only. However, the necessity occurred only on the few occasions when she reassured me that last noise meant nothing, or when I signaled her that the guards remained on their posts and weren't spreading out into the forest.

Tess and Sabine had granted themselves three hours for their exploration. It would leave them sufficient time to examine the periphery and snoop out various kinds of security installations, to study the guards' behavior, and to find out some details about the lodge itself.

After four hours at the latest, the two would pick us up. If they didn't show up, we had to assume they had been caught, and we would initiate the respective alternate plan. That alternate plan had to work mostly without discoveries about the area, and was designed to be accordingly robust.

In case our access had to happen earlier, we had another robust alternate plan.

Robust in this case meant *fast and venomous* — like our namesake.

The guard in my palm image was peacefully leaning against the railing of the lodge's rear entrance landing. The light plasma rifle was leaning against the doorframe. His pistol holster was heavily tearing at his left shoulder. He pulled at it from time to time.

His earpiece seemed to fit uncomfortably, too. Since we

had begun our observation, he had removed and replaced the item six times. Or was he just bored?

As unattentively as he performed his guard duty, I probably could've done a tap dance before the landing without being noticed. But his laxity might well be misleading. He had an athletic body, and his weapons seemed to be well-tended.

Now his head jerked up, and he placed one hand at his ear, listening. Then he reached for his gun.

I lifted my left hand, clenched to a fist, gaining Elodie's undivided attention.

The hiss of a plasma shot echoed around the building, and then—an ultrasonic whistle, only audible with special equipment. *Action!*

Elodie didn't need my sign. She had heard the whistle, too. But I was the one who had been watching the guard, so he was my target.

I rose, drew my pistol, leveled, and shot.

CHAPTER FIFTEEN

A shot across three hundred meters with a conventional pistol would be ineffective, with a standard plasma pistol nearly impossible, with our special, personal arms a challenge — and for a Mamba, for whom any failure during her training would have meant death, it was a difficult but solvable task.

In principle, I only had to score. A plasma ball caused so much damage to an unprotected target that precision didn't matter.

It did matter to me. So I was miffed about my shot hitting one span too high, burning my victim's throat away.

What's done is done — and we were running. Elodie had collected my equipment. Now it was all about our target.

The lodge had one long two-story residential wing and a service wing for kitchen, dining area, and the surgery — from our location behind the residential wing. The main entrance was where the two wings met.

Tess, Sabine, Gwen, and Avril had advanced toward the main entrance. Justine and Tia covered the service wing's far end.

The main entrance teams would split as planned and come toward us, or Justine and Tia, respectively, while we worked our way through the building from the outer ends. That meant Elodie and I had to pick one floor each — she upstairs, I downstairs. We had to make do without mutual cover inside.

One leap carried me over the railing and to the door. One foot pushed my victim's arm out of the way. Elodie positioned herself to the other side and nodded.

I placed my left hand on the knob and pulled at the heavy steel door. The snapper yielded with a click. Once I could push my foot through the gap, I took my hand back, drew the second pistol from its holster, and then pushed the door wide open with my foot.

Elodie shot right away — twice. Then she jumped through the door and pressed her back to a wall until I had followed her.

Nothing stirred at the corridor's far end. Whoever might linger around the lobby was sufficiently warned by the two lifeless bodies not to peek around the corner.

I passed the stairs and moved to the first door to the left. Elodie showed me another smile and then quietly hurried up the stairs with cat-like elegance.

Okay. One pistol back to the holster, hand to the door handle, open the door, glance left-right — empty. Jump forward and turn — no, nobody hiding behind the door. Under the neatly dressed bed? In the wardrobe? Back to the door, quick glance at the corridor — still clean.

I repeated the same game with the opposite room and then the next three, in turn one to the left, one to the right of the corridor. Neither one appeared to be in use.

This changed with the next room to the right — here I found a travel bag in the corner, trousers over the backrest, socks and a book lying on the floor next to the chair. But the guest wasn't present.

Together with the plasma rifles' hiss, now the characteristic bellows of several pistols echoed from the lobby. From that, I concluded Tess couldn't have made it to the building yet. If the guards could keep a team of four Mambas from reaching the lodge, they had to be darn good!

Under these circumstances, and because I didn't know anything about Justine and Tia, the life of our target could depend on Elodie and me — in the worst case on me alone if my partner was delayed on the upper floor.

I had to hurry up, and I couldn't make any mistakes. In this situation, I couldn't afford to miss something or someone, and then be taken by surprise by an enemy at my back.

Seven more doors. Quickly, but diligently, I searched the next rooms — to the left, to the right, to the left —

The young girl squealed in terror when I pushed the door open, and pulled up the bed cover.

Her terror could be genuine or a trick. After my quick glances behind the door, under the bed, and into the wardrobe, I tore her cover away. No, she surely couldn't hide a gun there.

"Get out!" I barked at her. "To the back!"

Despite my command, I stepped into the corridor first, and indeed, someone was just poking his head around the corner to the right — and a hand with a pistol.

Before I could shoot, my new target had already retreated into the cover of the wall. I pulled the naked girl through the door and pushed her down the corridor, and then I drew my second weapon.

A dark figure jumped over the two dead at the corridor end and broke through the last door to the left — before I could shoot, he had disappeared. *Merde!*

The next moment, head and hand reappeared, and I saw the muzzle flash.

CHAPTER SIXTEEN

A bullet hit the doorframe behind the position I had occupied right before. *If the enemy spotted you, move.*

My plasma round almost seared the ends of my opponent's hair and hit the quarry stone wall at the corridor's end. *Missed!*

A long leap almost took me to the door, and a second through it diagonally, whereby I turned toward the assumed shooter's position. But he was no longer inside this room. The wide open window indicated his escape path.

No, friend. If I stick my head outside, you'll punch a hole into it. I won't fall for that.

Instead I made a long leap outside — only backward, facing the lodge and pointing my guns at it, prepared to take the building's entire length under fire. Had he moved left, toward the main entrance, or right, toward our rear entrance?

A movement at one of the upper floor's windows made me dodge by reflex, and again, a pistol bullet missed me. The same kind of pistol, the noise told me. *If the enemy spotted you, move.*

I shot twice running, and the shape in the window disappeared. *Damn, Elodie was roaming up there!*

Doubtlessly she had heard the shots, too, but that was no reason to dump my problems on her, and a single guy with a gun was no match for a Mamba — even though this one here was quite good.

He was very good. A single, boosted jump carried me through the upper floor window, and I was ready to serve him a plasma round, but he wasn't in that room anymore.

A hiss and another shot sounded from the corridor, and I heard the crack of another room door and how someone inhaled with a wheeze — as Elodie sometimes did when she was very tense and didn't pay heed to this dangerous bad habit.

I announced myself with a whistle, so that she wouldn't shoot me — another avoidable noise, but in this case the lesser evil. Then I stepped into the corridor and looked right. Elodie stood in the next doorframe at my side. Of the diagonally opposite room's door — between the two of us — only fragments were dangling from the hinges.

My business, I indicated.

I made two quick steps and jumped through the door, then kicked myself forward right away. A shot bellowed and missed me before another bullet hit the wooden floor close to my foot.

I caught a brief impression of his surprised face over the length of my gun barrels before my plasma round burned his head away. No need for the second shot — he hadn't been able to dodge anymore.

My task here was completed, and there were three more unchecked rooms waiting on my level, so I hurried back to the room I had come through, jumped outside through the window, let myself drop until I could get hold of the lower room's window-frame, and swung myself back into the room — gaining obstructed sight through the door of the lobby area with several men standing behind pillars or cowering behind toppled tables, firing to where I knew the main door to be.

If Tess and Sabine hadn't advanced further yet, it was because they didn't dare to shoot inside blindly. It would have been an inexcusable mishap to accidentally hit our mission's objective.

That problem didn't apply to me, as I had a free firing

range and clearly recognizable targets. Five quick plasma shots later, the shooters were dealt with, and I stepped into the lobby entrance.

There, only one young lady had taken cover behind the masonry fireplace. When she spotted me, she closed her eyes in resignation.

CHAPTER SEVENTEEN

It didn't take long before Tess, Gwen, and Avril responded to the missing defense and entered the lodge. I nodded at them and turned to my remaining rooms.

I found no further opponents there, only one more scantily-clad entertainer, who I sent out to fetch her colleague. Thereafter, I returned to the lobby.

Elodie was about to fetch a nanomed compression bandage and treat Sabine's injured arm. She nodded toward the stairs. "Tess went upstairs. The target is in the OR with Justine, treating two injured girls."

I turned to the woman at the fireplace, who was watching me with teary eyes and didn't dare to speak. "You may come with us if you like—and wherever you like to go. This facility will be shut down."

"What's your name?" Sabine asked.

"H-Helen."

"Helen. That's a pretty name, Helen." Sabine raised her arm so that Elodie could check the bandage again. "Helen, you needn't be afraid. Monique, take the poor thing in your arms."

If Sabine considered that appropriate, I wouldn't disagree. I stepped closer to Helen and reached out my arms. She hesitated, but then took my hands so that I could pull her close. When I held her tight with my arms wrapped around her, I could feel rows of hard knots on her back—scar tissue.

"You should come with us," I whispered. "We can help you."

"Nobody can," she returned. "They'll come and get me."

"*They* are all dead."

"The bosses — the Syndicate."

"They can no longer hurt you."

I heard steps on the stairs and looked round. Gwen came first, followed by three more young women, and Avril accompanied a mid-fortyish man with blond curls. Tess and Justine formed the rear.

The man spotted Helen and me and came toward us with open arms. I allowed him to take her away from me.

"All will be good, Helen," he said. "All will be good. We're going to the Dragons. There you'll be safe."

Chapter Eighteen: Ariette

Of Zoé, only her pretty butt and her legs were visible, the rest remained hidden behind the weapon bay door of her Tigershark.

I waited with patience until she had unwound herself from the uncomfortable position under the plane. She smiled at me.

"Are we going again already?"

"Tess is still somewhat angry about the girls." I shrugged and pointed at the trees around Velvet Island's small landing platform. "We can't save all the world, she says, but we can't stay on vacation in paradise either while we know of more victims out there."

"Like Helen."

"They all suffered. With some, you can see it, for others it's more inside the head, and that's not as easy to fix for our nanos."

"Jo's good at that." Zoé pressed a hidden switch, and the door began to close.

"Jo's busy. We're there to solve her problems and not burden her with new ones."

"Yes." For one moment, Zoé stared a hole into the sky. Then she gave a start, approached me, and shoved me toward the community center. "You're right. Come, we'll grab an iced tea from Nanette, and then we'll hear what Tess is up to this time."

Elodie joined us when we took the turn to *our* stretch of the beach. Somehow it had turned out like this—the island's eastern tip was reserved for the lovers, the north-western beach around the community center served as retreat for our researchers and ecologists, and a small section in the north-east was considered our meeting area. The partially rocky south shore was reserved for the birds.

We briefly hugged each other, then we walked out onto the smooth sand hand-in-hand.

I believe that only we Mambas can understand the tight connection that ties us to each other and especially to our tandem partners. We learned the hard way that we can only survive together. We've seen our peers die until only the strongest, the fastest, the smartest, those with the best self-control remained — until only the best tandem teams could survive. We learned to be one body and one soul. We're mutual comfort and support, sparring partner and whipping girl. We know precisely how our partners think and act. *March separated, strike together* — that works without prior consultation. What's binding us is more intimate than sex.

This mental bond isn't easy to replace — such would require empathy like Johanna's, or a Dragon cock.

Therefore, Zoé will always remain an outsider to our group — a welcome outsider, but never part of a tandem team.

She understood. She wasn't mad at us for it. We didn't exclude her — we just couldn't integrate her as tightly as our respective tandem partners. Aside from that, we very well knew we could depend on the little lioness, the Knight of the Order of the Dying Lioness.

So she trudged along behind us, single, but not lonesome.

The healed wound on Sabine's upper arm was pale still, and Sabine appeared miffed where she was sitting in the sand. She didn't like having caught that hit at all, but all our training couldn't help against the power of fate and a stray bullet.

Tess showed her usual imperturbability.

"Okay, gals," she began. "Only the five of us this time. The target area is open, and according to our data, our instrument is poorly guarded. It's possible that we will strike right away again once conditions are favorable."

"How open exactly is the area?" Zoé asked.

"About the same as Velvet Island, only more rocky. The mansion sits on one of these remarkable rocks in the Vietnamese sea, in the Ha Long Bay. We'll have to swim and climb a bit."

Elodie smirked. My partner loved to swim. For me, it was just a pleasant exercise, and the reef was an interesting extra to our training, but she took to water like the proverbial fish.

"How exactly will we get there?" I asked. "By drop?"

Tess shook her head. "No. I'd rather have us deployed under water. Zoé, the Tigershark can dive, can't it?"

"Yes, but we don't have an airlock."

I could see our pilot disliked the idea of a plane full of ocean water.

"If you can expand the envelope field until we're all outside, and then cut it, we've got no trouble, right?" Tess asked. "Getting back in is the hard part."

"Yes, that should work."

CHAPTER NINETEEN

A solo man walked out on the beach from the palms and stopped, showing embarrassment and a slight bulge in his swimmers.

"Peter!" Tess greeted him happily. "Come over."

"Uh, yes." He trudged through the sand toward us. Again and again, his gaze slid across us, then to the side, as if he didn't know where to look.

Tess walked up to him and linked arms. "Don't be shy. You needn't be embarrassed. On Velvet Island, men may openly show their appreciation for the sight of well-shaped female bodies—if they want to. In any case, you needn't look away. Everyone may enjoy what we're showing."

"Well."

"That's different to the lodge," Sabine explained. "Women were reduced to lust objects there. Such a thing can't happen here—but that doesn't mean we may not feel lust, and moreover it doesn't mean we'd oppose male admiration. Or that we'd regard a firm erection as an insult. Just the opposite, right, gals?"

"I thought—I heard about your past. The Cartel drilled you." Peter stared down on Tess's and his own naked feet. "Wasn't that also—" He stopped.

"You mean if they raped us?" Sabine asked.

Peter nodded.

"No. Not us. They didn't have to. We craved for sex, day and night. The stuff they gave us, the stuff that made us stronger, made us hot, too. But we had a choice who we

52

would fuck, and they respected that—they had to respect that. You can't take a Mamba against her will."

We others nodded.

Elodie picked up the cue. "Sure, those who wouldn't toe the line were *sorted out.* A quick death—anything else wouldn't have been possible. Only we were still very nervous back then, all of us. The dosage had to be finetuned, and we had to work hard to keep our self-control. Such an act of violence—rape—could have triggered an undesired reaction. The girl in question would've been dead—but the man as well. Too risky. So they only offered themselves and took what they could get, or found relief with the other women outside the program."

Peter remained silent.

However easily we had met on this paradise beach, I found it difficult to comprehend our past situation. From here, it all appeared so wrong, so twisted, so unreal!

Tess placed one arm around Peter's hip and snuggled up to him. "That's over. This is paradise. Naked bodies are beautiful. Sex is beautiful. This is about passion, not about domination. Guys who think differently wouldn't feel comfortable here."

Sabine eyeballed Peter's swimmers. "We're helping each other. That's the core point. It's dragonish."

Peter, still embarrassed, placed one hand at his waistline. "You mean I should drop my pants?"

"Only if you already slapped coral extract on. Otherwise you'd burn your best piece." Tess took his hand up and placed it on her breast. "But you may touch, too, not just look."

Peter didn't pull his hand away.

"I'm still not over what you did at the lodge."

"What exactly do you mean?"

"Don't get me wrong. I'm grateful you got me and my

assistants out from there — and the other entertainers, too. But that would have been police business. That you simply . . ."

"That we simply killed the guards," Sabine completed his sentence and rubbed the pale spot on her arm. "That's our job. We're assassins, that's what we learned. We're proficient in killing."

"It so doesn't fit . . ."

"This paradise?" Tess asked. "No. We're not the cute mermaids. But we're no ice-cold killers, either — it only looks like that. During a mission, it may not be otherwise. We must decide in advance if such action is appropriate, and afterward we must stand by this decision and take responsibility for what we did."

Sabine looked straight up to his face. "For your mission, like on other occasions, we had decided to kill the guards in case of an escalation. There was an escalation."

"Who grants you the right to make such a decision?"

"The police force had its opportunity," Tess said. "For years. While you were kept imprisoned and the criminals just used young women up. It would be too easy to charge police and justice with failure."

"You could have told the police."

"We *should* have, you wanted to say. No. The police didn't just fail. They knew, and they looked away. They allowed the criminals to abuse our *protected* — some of the girls weren't even grown up yet!"

"Nevertheless," Peter insisted. "It's also a matter of principle."

"You're absolutely right there," Sabine chimed in again. "The law enforcement forces come first. It doesn't help our mission to destabilize working structures. We may not. Jo clearly instructed us — we may not roam around to kill people. Human laws prohibit that, and Dragon laws prohibit that, and the contracts between humans and Dragons prohibit it, too."

Peter frowned, but let Sabine go on.

"Nevertheless we do it—is that a contradiction? No, because there are clear exceptions. We may defend our lives, and we may defend other people if they can't do it on their own. We may fight piracy and terrorism, and we may free hostages. If organized crime keeps people imprisoned, we may start a rescue mission—and in this case, all crime organization members are legitimate targets, as a matter of principle."

"Which you implement by force."

"Only if we can't avoid it. If possible, we rescue our targets quietly. If necessary, we'd rather let the police beat us up and rape us than start a war. Ask Monique if you want to know more."

"Rape?" He gazed at me in shock.

I shrugged. "A minor sacrifice, compared to the life of a police officer. After all, they're our *protected,* too."

"But that—" The words failed him.

"I'm not one of the weak, so I restrain myself as long as my life isn't at stake—even if I could have easily defeated the police officer. That's *our* principle, and that's what we're fighting for—every way necessary."

CHAPTER TWENTY

We didn't get to see much of the almost two thousand limestone isles in Ha Long Bay because Zoé submerged her Tigershark for the last leg of our journey.

Only after leaving her vessel, when we briefly surfaced for orientation, could we cast a quick glance on some of the densely covered limestone pillars. Elodie and I couldn't linger and admire them, as our schedule was tight. Because Tess and Sabine took a different route, and because we had opted against any kind of radio signals, we had to dive toward our target without delay.

Propeller noise approached us from ahead. Elodie and I glanced at each other. *Surface and check,* I signaled.

Elodie poked her head out first, I followed.

Instead of patiently waiting for our rescue mission — of which he didn't know, of course — in his luxury accommodation, our target came to us in a small motorboat. He wasn't even accompanied by guards. Neither of us would have expected that!

We quickly dove down again and faced each other.

Abandon mission? Elodie signaled.

Negative, I replied and placed one finger on my protective suit's collar. One moment later, the suit opened down to my crotch and loosened around my arms and legs. I brushed the nano fiber off with few trained moves, scrunched it up and handed the bundle to my partner. Lastly, I left my breather to her. Then I surfaced and swam toward the boat.

The driver reduced speed and waited patiently until I had pulled myself over the side with both hands and found a comfortable seat facing him.

"You shouldn't be here," he said with a friendly smile.

"Robert Jacob Wilson?" I asked.

"Yes?" Now he frowned.

"I'm Monique. According to my information, you're held captive against your will here by the Cartel. Does that apply?"

He relaxed. "No. It's been so in the past, yes, but the Cartel no longer exists."

I leaned forward. His glance briefly touched my figure, and then he gazed out on the sea again.

"You already know that? There you're way ahead of many other Dragon technology experts."

"Oh, Dragon technology. That was a long time ago."

"But that's what you were held for."

He closed his eyes. "That's the past. Back then . . . I decided to forgo this knowledge." Now he fixed his gaze on me. "I decided to be of no use to anyone any longer and focus on my hobby."

"The birds."

"You're remarkably well informed."

"That's my job."

He squinted. "What exactly is your job?"

"To rescue people."

"Who are versed with Dragon technology."

"Yes."

"By order of whom?"

"I'm working for the Imperatrix Aurea Draconis, Johanna Meier."

"Never heard of her."

That was something new. "Meier effect?"

"I've heard about that."

"She founded a new university."

"Under whose reign?"

"Velvet Island is sovereign Dragon territory."

"There are no Dragons anymore."

I leaned back and smiled. "If you know that for sure."

That made him think. "They all departed. Back then."

"Everyone thought so."

Now he shrugged. "Who cares? That doesn't matter to me. Or does it?" He cocked his head.

"It's your decision. I can only make you an offer. We need teachers and researchers to prepare for the second wave."

"Second wave?"

"Jellies. The Invasion."

"Oh, that. We won't stand a chance there anyway."

Now it was my turn to frown. "So you didn't hear about that? It was just last year we killed a mothership. Only, that wasn't the second wave yet."

"What are you saying, killed a mothership? No bomb in the world would be strong enough—"

"I can't explain the details, but somehow you can modify an envelope field to make it shatter solid matter. A derivation of the Meier effect."

Robert gazed at me with renewed interest. "What do you know about that?"

"Too little. But I don't have to. I must collect people who want to join us. Do you want to reconsider?"

He shook his head. "No. I'm done with that topic. Thank you for your efforts, good luck with your future plans, and if you meet someone who remembers me, you may relay greetings. I prefer to stay with my birds." He nodded past me. "There they come. I told you that you shouldn't be here. I'm sorry."

Two patrol boats of the North Vietnamese navy just came around one of the picturesque rocks—way too close!

"You don't have to be sorry," I only said and let myself slip into the water backward.

CHAPTER TWENTY-ONE

The four uniformed men per patrol boat hadn't looked friendly with their rifles, and their reaction to my roll into the water matched — while I was making my first swimming stroke, some of them opened fire.

I must have been lucky that those first shots were poorly aimed, nevertheless one of them hit my left leg above the ankle.

The impact shock made me briefly see stars, not to mention the biting pain, and that alone instantly told me I wouldn't want to let them capture me.

Just go! I activated my booster and dove deeper *fast*, as much as my injured leg allowed. Each swimming stroke sent new waves of pain up my leg, and at the same time I felt my power fade — the blood loss had to be significant.

Sadly, I hadn't brought anything along to treat my wound. The only thing missing now would be a shark.

I heard the propeller sounds above me and saw the boats' shadows circle. Thoughts of blood loss, pain, potential capture, interrogation, torture, the risk of unveiling the mission circled in my head.

A flash! The next moment, a shockwave caught me and spun me around. The Vietnamese had launched a hand grenade!

I'd almost lost my consciousness. But my booster not only made me fast, it also kept me awake. Hence I saw the slender shape coming toward me and prepared for defense.

It was no shark, it was Elodie. She forced the breather into my mouth and took my arms, pulled them around her neck.

I held tight, and she accelerated. The next grenade's shockwave only caressed us.

Elodie slowed down and tried to give me my suit. I pointed at my leg, where every heartbeat pumped new blood into the sea.

My partner nodded, took the nano suit and knotted it tightly around my leg. Then she fetched a bandage from her own suit belt and wrapped it around the wounds.

The blood flow stopped instantly, and shortly after that, the pain faded. I only felt weak.

Now I allowed her to untie the suit and pull it around me so that it could protect me against sharks and further shots.

I gratefully acknowledged her next signal—*I'll pull you along.* Maybe I could've mustered the power myself, but I felt very drained, and my partner hadn't made a real effort so far, aside from a brief booster phase. Moreover, the nanomed bandage fed on my reserves, too.

Two more explosions flashed in short sequence—close enough to make us feel the shockwaves. Our chasers seemed eager to eliminate the fish population in this part of the bay entirely—in a world heritage area! If that was standard procedure, I shouldn't be surprised about the lack of sharks.

Elodie wasn't troubled. She continued pulling me along toward our meeting point. We simply assumed Tess and Sabine had noticed the mission abort.

CHAPTER TWENTY-TWO

Tess didn't say a word. Not when we arrived at the meeting point and not when we mounted the camouflaged Tigershark. She was still silent when Zoé announced that we had reached our travel altitude. Our leader didn't even give me the look.

I was the one to finally break the silence. "He wouldn't come along."

"You talked with him?" she asked with genuine surprise.

"The opportunity was favorable," I said after a glance at my partner. "The risk of meeting his guards was zero. The patrol was surprisingly early, though."

"We'll check whether they changed the tour, it was pure chance, or they'd been warned," Tess decided. "But first tell me your report."

I did that, from the moment we spotted our target to our arrival at the meeting point. Tess made a worried face when I mentioned my injury but didn't interrupt me.

"You could've pretended to surrender and eliminated the patrol," Tess said. "That might have been less risky."

"Maybe," I admitted. "But this way they — the target and the patrol — only saw a foreign naked woman and not a superfast warrior who can take out an entire patrol boat crew on her own."

"Was that the reason you stripped the suit off?"

"The less we unveil, the less Jo has to explain. Moreover, I thought he'd feel less threatened if I appeared without the suit."

Our leader smiled. "Yes, that was a good decision." Then she frowned. "Are you okay?"

She must have seen something before I noticed it myself, but then my world turned black.

CHAPTER TWENTY-THREE

Tender warm lips parted from mine, followed by a deep breath by my partner. I wrought a flutter from my eyelids.

"She's back," Sabine commented, and Elodie pulled her head further back.

I was no longer sitting in my seat, but lying on the floor in the narrow aisle.

"How do you feel?" Elodie asked.

"I don't know." I tried to raise an arm. It required some effort. "Weak. Dizzy."

"Did you lose much blood?" Tess asked out of the back.

"No—yes—I don't know. Probably yes. After the hit I had to dive deep first, then came the grenade, then Elodie pulled me away."

"The wound looked ugly," Elodie added. "Shot right through the lower leg, and I couldn't tell if the bone was hit."

"That can use up a lot of healing power," Tess said. "Add the loss of blood, and you used booster, too, right?"

"Yes."

"So your reserves were already down, and the nanos simply take what they need. You're empty. Elodie, she needs an access."

"At once." My partner rose.

Meanwhile, I heard Tess's voice from the cockpit. "Monique must go into the tank. Please step on it and call the island."

"I'll do. Everything secured?"

"No—Sabine's just placing a catheter."

64

"Oh. Better finish that before I give you a good shaking."

"Hey, are you still there?"
Elodie slapped my cheek.
"Hmmm?"
"You were gone again. Don't kid around, yes? Try to stay awake until we've got you in the tank, okay? Zoé will hurry."
She was sitting right next to me and above me. I felt belts around my upper arms and turned my head to the side. Everything started to spin around me.
I fought for my consciousness, and a while later, the nausea faded. Now I could see the belts knotted to the seat supports. It didn't look very professional, but as long as it prevented me from being tossed across the cabin, I gladly overlooked that.
I lifted my head up again very slowly. Only now I did I notice the padding under my head. I also noticed the growing pain in my leg.
"Ouch!"
Sabine leaned down from the other side of the aisle. "The leg, right? That's a good sign—the healing nanos have done their job. They're allowing normal nerve impulses to pass again. It also means they won't drain your resources anymore. I can give you a painkiller if you can't stand the pain, but right now I'd rather not burden your circulation with it."
"No, all right." I tried to suppress the pain with autosuggestion. Otherwise the sting in my leg at least kept me awake.
No matter how fast Zoé flew—it became a long journey for me.

Chapter Twenty-four: Aria Di Portamento

The bench was hard and uncomfortable, the edgy backrest pummeled my back with every bump in the road, the frosty wind wheezed through the canvas cracks, crept through all the winter clothing's layers, and made me shiver.

"Are you all right?" Elodie asked for what felt like the one-hundred-and-first time from the opposite bunk.

"Speak Russian," Tia immediately warned her and in that language.

"I'm fine," I assured them—of course in Russian, too. We hadn't had much time to slip into this role and refresh our Russian, so it was advisable to stay in character. "It's just fucking cold."

Elodie grinned and switched language, too. "Not acclimatized yet?"

"Not at all."

"You girl."

I grinned back and mocked a fist-strike—and could just about hold my arm back when our truck scuttled over a road bump and tossed us all around.

"Whew," Lucy uttered when the next bump lifted us from our seats and firmly dropped us on our benches again, while the antique army vehicle's suspension crashed into its stops.

My teeth chattered hard as my butt couldn't entirely cushion the impact, but I suppressed a curse. In the even white outside, Gwen had a hard time recognizing the road, not to mention spotting any bumps. I didn't want to know how many potholes she spotted in time to spare us.

The army coats over our uniforms should actually keep us warm, but the effect was limited. Sadly, our proposals for improvement had been turned down. Our entire equipment had to be absolutely authentic—should we have to leave something or someone behind, there could be no trace leading back to the University.

For the same reason, Tess and Sabine couldn't accompany us—both had appeared in public too often and might be known to the Russian authorities.

Justine, Tia's partner, had assumed the lead for this mission instead. She sat next to Gwen and Avril in the tight but heated cab, and on a cushioned seat.

Tia had left the third seat to Avril and joined us in the back. Aside from Lucy, Elodie, and myself, *us* included Lucy's partner Laura and Yvette and Kim—ten of the sixteen Mambas working for Jo. Beate had left the team after Jasmine's death to stay with Freddie on his boat, and Francine, Sylvie, and Zoé had their pilot jobs.

There were too few of us to fulfill our primary role of protecting the island against spies and terrorists and going on such missions. But not one of us wished any other girl in the world a training like the one we had survived, so there wouldn't be any more Mambas ever. The only other graduates had opposed Jo in Marseille and Paris and hadn't survived this confrontation.

CHAPTER TWENTY-FIVE

"Oops," Tia commented on our vehicle's most recent hop. "So, gals, we'll be there soon. Check each other's uniforms and equipment once again. We're playing a special unit, so there can't be any slack or we're busted faster than a Dragon at Footy."

I had a loose comment on the tip of my tongue as I imagined our Achrotzyber at Australian football, but I swallowed it. For one, this subject didn't fit into our role at all, and for two, it was time to act the professional.

A good deal more than during the other missions, here in Siberia it was about avoiding attention. Jo had trouble enough with the Russians, so we shouldn't add fuel to the fire.

So I diligently checked my partner's impeccable fit of uniform, coat and faux fur cap, her shiny boot polish and shiny linear assault rifle, just like she checked my appearance.

She couldn't check my fitness, and her worries about that were written on her face. "I'm unconditionally mission-ready," I assured her once again. "No aftereffects, neither physical nor mental."

"Any problem, Elja?" Tia immediately investigated.

"No, Lieutenant," my partner hurried to say.

"Good. Effective immediately, we're in the drill, phase two. Masks."

Elodie handed me her rifle and pulled the thin insulation masks from the rim of her cap down over her chin. The glacier visor followed, and then she took both our rifles so that I could do the same. Again, we mutually checked each other.

Tia got help from Lucy and then knocked at the back of the cab. We were ready.

CHAPTER TWENTY-SIX

The truck stopped, and I had to suppress the impulse to also stop breathing. It was time to get down to business.

Footsteps crunched in the snow, came closer. Our vehicle's right door opened, and there was another crunch when Justine exited.

"What are you doing here? Get gone!" a harsh male voice ordered.

"I am Colonel Julia Iwanowa. This is an installation of the Russian armed forces, and I demand immediate admittance."

"You *demand?*"

That was the cue for Tia. She waved at us, and I pulled the canvas's rear latch open. Elodie jumped out first, I followed, then the other Mambas, and Tia last.

Like a clockwork, we found our place in the line and assumed attention instantly. Tia nodded in approval, said, "Deploy," and advanced.

Lucy and Laura followed her around the driver's side. Yvette and Kim hurried to the right, and Elodie and I went into position behind Justine, our barrels aiming at the ground.

Now we could have a look around. Our truck was parked before a closed boom gate. A barrack cowered into the snow to the right, black garbage bags were piled up on the left. The area, with two flat garage buildings and a bunker entrance made of meters deep concrete, was encompassed by two-meter-high netting wire topped with barbed wire.

One guard peeked out of the barrack window, and the boom as well as the bunker entrance were covered by several cameras. The cameras and the access road were meticulously kept clear of snow and ice.

A lone man in a black duvet jacket, with the inevitable fur cap and with a plasma pistol in his gloved hand, stood between our truck and the boom and tried in vain to stare Justine down.

Our appearance turned the odds clearly to his disadvantage. He looked like he had noticed that.

"I *demand*," Justine confirmed. "I'm informed that you procured an *exclusive right of use* for this station and don't want to be disturbed. But I assure you, it's in your interest if we can accomplish our mission soon."

"Why?"

"A data reconciliation showed that the station might not have been completely cleared upon shutdown. We're here to collect the remnants before there's an accident."

"Remnants? Accident?"

"You might be sitting on top of an armed nuclear warhead that's slowly rusting away, and one day . . ." She placed her fingertips together and let them snap away upward.

Her opponent paled.

"I don't care what you're doing here. I just want to pick up the warhead and get away with it as fast as possible."

"Oh. Well, yes, I'll ask. One moment, please." He quit his hopeless attempt of blocking our way and hurried back to the barrack entrance.

After he made a brief, flourishing exchange with his colleague, the boom opened.

Gwen quickly started our truck, and we followed on foot. Thus began phase three.

CHAPTER TWENTY-SEVEN

Lucy and Laura pushed the heavy, almost coffin-sized crate to the edge of the cargo bed, where Elodie and I took over. The moment I had to bear the full burden I sensed a dim dragging pain in my left calf. Grinding my teeth, I held out until Lucy and Laura had left the truck and took their part of the load. After all, we didn't want to show a weakness before the guards—ideally they shouldn't even notice that there were women beneath all these thick winter uniforms, after that couldn't be avoided with Justine and Tia.

The four of us hauled the crate to the bunker entrance. Justine went ahead with Yvette, while Tia and Kim formed the rear. In this order, we also entered the poorly lit downhill hallway behind the thick steel door.

Gwen and Avril stayed behind to guard our truck and keep the guards from silly ideas.

After strenuous twenty meters under the surveillance cameras' eyes, we reached a cargo elevator. There we could set our burden down.

Justine watched Tia press the Down button with a stern face, then gave the look to any of us who dared to wiggle as much as a finger.

Yvette and Kim were keeping their firearms ready, but still pointing down, when the elevator stopped at the underground floor. The rest of us had lifted the crate before the steel doors slid open.

The adjacent bunker room was two stories high and about twenty-five meters deep and twelve meters wide. Numerous rows of LEDs provided even lighting. Several red-painted hooks hung down from crane rails at the ceiling, and the racks along the walls were stuffed with barrels, small containers, and pressure canisters.

Five men were blocking our way so that we couldn't leave the elevator — four baldheads with plasma pistols flanked one seemingly unarmed giant, and they all made a big effort to appear grim. Their checkered camouflage suits and combat boots underlined the martial impression.

Justine wouldn't let that disturb her. She stepped up to the giant and focused on his face. "I am Colonel Iwanowa. We need access to the G corridor."

A vein at the giant's temple pulsed visibly, but otherwise his face remained emotionless when he replied. "The terms for take over this location didn't provide for inspections."

"We haven't come for an inspection. We're here to correct a mistake."

"You weren't announced."

"Of course not. This mission is secret. I'm authorized to inform you about the potential existence of expired nuclear warheads in this facility, though."

"Define *expired.*"

"The possibility of a leak, of overheating or melting with subsequent chemical and radioactive contamination of this facility can no longer be ruled out — the likelihood increases with the duration of its stay."

"Where exactly is the warhead stored?"

"The warheads — should such indeed have been left behind upon this station's shutdown — are located in a part of the G corridor not accessible to you. Details are secret and do not affect your right of use for this location."

"I must not let you pass."

"I won't be refused admittance. I will fulfill my mission with your agreement or without."

The giant didn't look irritated. "You're looking for trouble?"

"I'm looking for lost nuclear warheads, nothing else. No matter how many bribes you pay — this is still a Russian military facility. I'm entitled to be here, and you're not. I'm entitled to remove civilians from this facility. I have the rights and the means to enforce my orders — but honestly, what would you lose by letting us do our job? Nothing but a bomb ticking under your asses."

Until her last two placatory sentences, the tension in the four armed men had grown. Justine's deliberately friendly inflection calmed them down somewhat. We all stayed alert nevertheless — should the guards as much as bend their index fingers, we had to dodge *fast*.

Although I only had to bear a quarter of the weight, my leg complained about the strain again. I hoped the guys would *soon* be willing to accept a solution.

"Except for the G corridor, there's nothing in this facility I'm interested in," Justine went on. "I already know from our archive photos what the G corridor looks like. There's nothing in there you'd have to protect. You won't gain anything by dismissing us, either. Instead, we all can only lose if there's trouble."

From our perspective it was clear that the five men would at least lose their consciousness, if not their lives, and we might at most lose our mission's inconspicuousness. Our opponents would probably have an entirely different point of view — four of them had their fingers at the triggers of their plasma weapons, against two of us who'd first have to level their linear assault rifle barrels, was that a safe bet? They couldn't and shouldn't know anything about Mambas — or if they had heard of Mambas through the convoluted flows of information in the Cartel, they shouldn't make the connection with us.

Nevertheless, I admired the giant's demonstrated calmness. Even if he probably boiled under the quiet surface, he kept his exemplary countenance, just like Justine quietly waited for his reply.

So his voice slightly trembled when he finally said, "Well then. We'll accompany you into the G corridor."

He waved at one of his men. "Go ahead and make sure all side doors are closed."

The man turned around and hurried toward the third exit to the right. As soon as he was out of sight, the giant gave way. "Please."

CHAPTER TWENTY-EIGHT

We walked up the G corridor like a small funeral procession—Justine and Tia first, then we with our crate, behind us Yvette and Kim, followed by the giant and the other three men. The latter had at least lowered their gun barrels.

I pondered whether the giant might have a fever—when we passed him, he felt like a small oven.

Or had we taken him from the sauna? This thought in turn triggered an associative chain that led me to consider if his member was proportionally sized. I quickly called myself to order—*Professional focus on the task, gal!*

The G corridor led to a dead end—or at least it looked like that. Tia carefully shielded her partner against the forward guard's questioning glance, while Justine placed a small box against the concrete in the place where our instructions located the hidden induction sheet and then entered the code from the Cartel headquarters' database.

If the code was wrong or the mechanism didn't work, we'd not only have egg on our faces, but also have to leave empty-handed.

For one moment I thought *that's it.* Then a brief chime sounded.

There was a humming and crunching, and then the wall at the corridor end started to move sideways—only to a gap, whereupon Justine stopped the gate with another keypress and looked past us at the giant.

"The area beyond the gate is not your business. I must insist that you leave us now."

"What kind of box is that?"

"If I tell you, I must kill you."

"Oh, never mind." The giant turned around. "Guys, we're leaving."

I was surprised that he gave up so quickly. Of course, he had recognized that the secret part beyond the wall wasn't his area — and that we indeed had a good reason to be here.

Elodie saw the reason for his willingness to cooperate first. "Colonel," she whispered and focused on a bump in the corridor ceiling.

Justine followed my partner's gaze and pulled a small pistol from her coat. A single drop of paint from the gun obstructed the surveillance camera's view on the corridor end.

Only now did she let the gate open wide enough to let us pass with our crate. Yvette and Kim stayed behind as planned, and then Justine closed the secret access.

CHAPTER TWENTY-NINE

W e could assume that the secret underground corridor didn't contain surveillance equipment. Of course, this assumption was no reason for lack of discipline. Accordingly, we proceeded in silence—even though I occasionally felt a slight drag in my left leg.

The passage seemed to be endless. About every hundred meters it took a turn of ten to fifteen degrees, alternatingly to the right or to the left. From the briefing I knew we had to expect thirty such bends, but after a while I stopped counting.

Finally we reached another solid-looking wall. Only a small steel door at the side seemed to lead anywhere. Behind it, the plan showed the machine room for the gate.

Above us had to be the other barracks area, in the luxurious catacombs in which our target was kept captive. Before us, behind the gate, should be the research station where a long time ago, before the Invasion, a scientific elite had worked on improving the Russian nuclear potential.

Before us, behind the gate, our target should have worked on the improving the Cartel weapon potential—if she had been unconditionally willing to do so. According to our data, she had thrown the Cartel the occasional crumb but otherwise done little of what had been hoped for.

Before us, behind the gate, lay our mission's success or failure. If the adjacent corridor was under the same kind of camera surveillance as corridor G, we would fail. If our target person wasn't present, we would fail. If she was guarded, we would fail.

If she didn't want to come with us, we would fail, too. But we considered this very unlikely. The surroundings were simply too uncomfortable.

Justine placed her control element to the wall again and gazed at each of us in turn.

Tia leveled her gun. We others nodded.

Justine entered the code, and the heavy gate started moving with a rumble. From now on, every second counted — the noise couldn't go unnoticed.

We were lucky — the space on the other side was not under surveillance. However, someone had erected racks at our wall, and we had to move the crate across a quickly emptied shelf with caution.

Justine closed the passage behind us. The potential delay in case of a hasty retreat — with a failed mission then — counted little against the unlucky chance of someone spotting our presence only because of an open secret door.

For the same reason, we replaced the shelf contents. A cursory inspection of this room shouldn't reveal anything conspicuous. We couldn't restore the dust on the shelf, the lack of which a thorough examination would unveil. We had to live with that risk.

By raising the crate we told Justine we could proceed. A sting in the left leg at the same time told me I wasn't as well as I should be after the healing bath in the tank.

I didn't say anything. My leg was my problem alone. Justine and Tia were busy enough leading us through the bunker facility, concerns about my leg and my mission readiness would only bug them.

Tia opened the improvised storage room door to the corridor, Justine peeked through the crack, showed a thumbs-up, and then stepped outside. Tia followed, and last came our crate.

Our target had to be close. *Darn sting in my calf!* Only one more door ahead. Behind it should be the lab where she was doing her research during the day.

She didn't even turn her head when the door slid open. "What is it, Iljitsch?"

Her hands wandered across the table erratically, found a pencil, while she continued to lean over the eyepiece before herself.

"I am Justine."

The head rose slowly. "That's not a typical Russian name."

"Belgian. I come from Australia. Johanna Meier sends her greetings and invites you to visit her. If you don't want that, we'll gladly take you to any other place you tell us."

"Johanna Meier — the Meier effect?"

"Exactly."

"Should I swap one prison for another?"

"You're free to go anytime and anywhere you like. You can visit the University any time later."

"What university?"

"The Dragon technology university on Velvet Island, before the Queensland coast."

The woman straightened herself and swung around on her swivel chair, scrutinized us. "Who are you?"

"We are the ones who can free you from the Syndicate's grasp."

"So, can you do that?" She combed her partially grayed streaks with one hand. "Do you think one can simply amble out from here?"

"We've ambled in," Justine said. "There's a secret corridor that links this bunker with the neighboring missile silo, and the Syndicate doesn't know about it. Officially, we're here on behalf of the Russian army to salvage a forgotten nuclear warhead. Should we find one, surely no one will request to open its transport case." She pointed at the crate on our shoulders.

My leg itched.

"I shall hide in there?"

"Yes. The crate contains a breather. However, Peter Berg recommended a tranquilizer. It will be tight, dark and quiet inside. It's easier to bear while sleeping."

"Peter Berg? He still exists?"

"He sends his greetings. He also asked me to tell you that you needn't bring Soviet Champagne."

"No Soviet Champagne?" Suddenly a tear ran down her cheek — but she smiled. "Then it's true? You came to free me?"

CHAPTER THIRTY

The wooden framework rose from the sand in the lagoon like a messenger from a different time. When had it been used last? At high tide, you rowed a boat beneath it, pulled the cargo up, and at low tide, you lowered the cargo into the sand to carry it up to the beach.

Had the men who had carried the cargo back then been able to enjoy the wonderful sunsets? Had they suffered pain in their legs from the hard work?

Nanette leaned down to me and handed me a beer. "Here."

"Thanks," I said without looking up. "Got a moment?"

"Sure." She let herself sink into the sand. "How did it go?"

"According to the plan." I described our advance into the facility. "The end was kind of spooky. I mean, who likes to be put into a coffin? You can't move inside the inflated stuffing. But she took it with good countenance—and then she fell asleep. The way out was a walk in the park thereafter."

"Except for you."

"Except for me. An unforeseeable mental rejection reaction, Peter says. The leg was perfectly okay, but the pain still was hell."

"I don't know anything about that."

"No, of course. It's gone anyway. And I'll stay."

"Only for this mission."

"Says Tess, now. And then? Next time? *We don't need the whole team. Thank you, Monique, have a little rest.*"

Nanette remained silent.

"I feel so useless."

"Last time, Tess stayed here herself. Don't you think it's your turn once? Give the others a chance to catch up to you."

"Catch up to me?" I watched our community center's good soul at my side with a frown.

She smiled. "You are *good,* Monique. Better than your mates, and together with Elodie a reliable support for the team. Good enough that the other gals start to rely on you—and that's dangerous."

"Yes." If that was true, it was dangerous indeed. "Who claims so?"

"Tess—to Jo. Perhaps I shouldn't tell you, but on the other hand, it's no secret either. Where's Elodie, by the way?"

"She was in need of a cock."

"Ah. You're not?"

"Later, perhaps. For now, I needed some time to think." I raised the beer can and emptied it in one draft. "And for this."

"Another?" Nanette rose.

"Yes, thanks."

She placed one hand on my shoulder. "We're one team, Moni. Tess would openly tell you if something was wrong. Don't worry."

"Okay."

Chapter Thirty-one: Aria Di Sma-nia

Tess and Sabine both didn't look happy when they left the Tigershark. I put my box down and nodded at them. "Didn't go well?"

"In line with the plan," our leader replied. "We remained undetected. Three times."

"Three times?"

"The first two target locations were deserted — empty, no guards, no instrument, no traces left behind. Completely blank."

"So the targets are gone. That's sad."

"We found the targets again — at the third location. As it seems, they've been co-located recently, and the fortress will be a hard nut to crack. We should talk all together. Can you summon the others?"

"Sure." I pointed at my box. "I'm just delivering the mail for the research station, okay?"

"Okay. Why you?"

"I lost a bet."

"Ah, well. Let's say, in half an hour on the beach?"

"All right."

"'Til then."

The two went off. I picked up my box, hailed Zoé, who was now inspecting her plane, and hurried toward the ocean biology research station to honor the first part of my bet. Claude was surely already waiting for me.

One had to know about the fortress to immediately spot it, as form and color were very well matched to the mountain peak it was situated on. Without the few openings for light, airing, and massive steel doors, it could be taken for a massive piece of rock.

"How do you get in there?" Yvette asked and passed the photos on.

"From above," Tess answered and showed a big aerial photo. "What looks like massive rock from the side in fact is just the wall around the fortress. Up to the central tower, this wall winds around one and a half times, and between the walls you find nine open courtyards, separated by thinner walls. The next to last and largest courtyard offers enough space for a heliport, where the provisions are brought in."

She began to copy the photo into the sand with rough strokes. "This is the central tower. The wall starts here at eleven o'clock, follows the longish mountain shape in a wide arc clockwise to come close again between five and seven o'clock. Toward nine o'clock the wall rises once more and forms another larger open area before it subsequently, between eleven and seven o'clock, winds itself around its own inner sections again."

She added more strokes within the spiral sketch. "The inner walls separate the ninth courtyard at about one o'clock, the eighth at five o'clock, the seventh at seven o'clock, the sixth at eleven o'clock, and the others at one o'clock, two and four o'clock, five and seven o'clock. Well—the third courtyard sits above the steep mountain crag, and the four outer courtyards north and south also end right at the scarp face and are quite steep inside, too. Only the innermost four courtyards are somewhat even—with that heliport at the eighth and a reservoir inside the sixth."

Tess added a rectangle and an oval.

"The aerial doesn't show much of it," she admitted. "You can see the lake, and if you look close enough, you'll see some contours. But the photos also unveil the building's major weak point—there are almost no even walls. Almost everything is cut from the rock in such a way that it appears natural, and that makes the outer walls nicely edged—climbably edged. Gals, we'll have some training units in bouldering."

"Ropes are out of the question, are they?" Lucy asked.

"On the last leg, yes." Tess pointed at the outer contours. "Once we approach the outer walls, we must operate without safety. Until then, farther below, we can secure ourselves with rock-colored ropes—especially if we climb in the dark. But I don't want us to be spotted by a chance approaching helicopter."

"Where do we have to go?" Kim pointed at the tower. "Are they in there?"

"The tower harbors the only living quarters, yes—but there's a cellar. However, if they grant their guests a bit of daylight, we shouldn't have to deal with the cellars. According to the old data, there's only storage in those."

"What are they researching?" Kim asked.

Tess shrugged. "That's not entirely clear. The instrument originally located here, Gustave Aubertin, is specialized in ignition lasers within the fusion technology area. Song Qin Chao graduated in nano tool machines, and Filipa Lopes deals with compact batteries."

"I don't like the picture that's emerging," Elodie said.

Laura turned to her. "What are you worried about?"

"Tiny laser weapons that can be hidden in a pen or inside a sleeve."

"Oh."

"It will become a hot mission anyway," Tess explained. "The fortress is well guarded, and the guards are good—that's why we didn't go in. There are a few of the usual security measures, that is, cameras, spots, and barbed wire, but nothing expensive. Instead, the guards are well equipped. They have plasma pistols, even rifles, wear protective suits and helmets, and are wearing visor glasses, and we must assume they know how to use them."

Tia raised a hand. "What does that mean for our targets? Are they cooperating now? Would they still want to leave?"

"We can't be sure," Tess admitted. "Their walks may give a clue—we've spotted all three of them in the courtyard. Alone, always at the same time, and each time accompanied by two guards. Perhaps they're not even allowed to talk with each other."

"What's the point in bringing them together, then?" Tia asked. "Simpler logistics, tighter security, or a joint project?"

"It can be all. In any case, the fortress is less accessible than the two deserted locations, easier to shield, and you don't have to take research results outside of the protected area. Or maybe it's about applying more pressure? Like, if you don't toe the line, the others will suffer? We can't tell, but I expect our mission to be welcome."

Sabine drilled the last pin into the edge of the aerial photo. "So, and from here you've got the best view on the fortress."

"Thanks you." Tess rose and placed her hands on her hips. "I said it before, this will be a hot mission. We'll have to free three targets. It will be difficult enough to synchronize our access, and it will be even harder to remain unspotted. I expect it won't work. Therefore, we will go in with full gear—including radio, so that we can coordinate with each other. That means—nobody must get caught, nobody must stay behind."

Tia spoke up again. "What about witnesses?"

"Those don't worry me—but camera recordings do. We will wear masks. If there's enough time, I'd like to pay the surveillance central a visit."

"Where is it?"

Tess gave Elodie the look—mockingly. "Sadly, we don't know that."

"Then we should restrain ourselves, right?"

"Until we've eliminated the cameras, that would be better, yes—but more important than the cameras is that the guards won't get us." Tess smiled. "Even without our booster, we have some advantages. Let's talk about the task assignments now. Zoé, your role is obvious, you'll fly us—and you'll have to shield our plane. According to the tracks we found, there could be patrols."

"Uh, what do you mean?"

"If necessary, you'd have to take out such a patrol."

"You mean, I may fight?"

"You're part of the team, aren't you?"

Zoé beamed.

Rightly so—if I remembered rightly, that was the first time Tess called her that.

CHAPTER THIRTY-TWO

Don't look down.
Of course, I did it anyway.

Elodie's moonlit face smiled at me while a wild river rolled through the narrow high valley many hundred meters below her.

Go on.

I fetched a piton from my belt and probed the rock crack before my face with it. It felt as if it would hold.

A few beats with the noise-protection-coated hammer later I could attach a carabiner to it, feed my rope through the latter and — after a testing jolt — continue my climb.

When we had discussed the access path assignments and the climb across the steep northern rock face had come up, Tess had only briefly glanced at me, and I had volunteered. Yes, of course Elodie and I would do the hardest part, and of course we would arrive at the fortress wall base on time.

Of course.

It was in our nature — or in our job's nature — to accept the most dangerous tasks as day-to-day routines, like an offered cup of coffee, and it was in our nature to execute them calmly and diligently. There was no room for fear or doubt.

At least not during a mission. I searched for a new place for my right foot and relocated my weight. Next, I reached with my left for the ledge I had spotted before.

The rope was annoying. Before each move I had to ensure it couldn't get caught at a rock spur. Without the rope, Elodie and I could have advanced faster. Instead, we could only climb in turns, had to pause every now and then apply a piton and thread our rope.

The risk of a fall was low. Elodie and I were good climbers, and the rock face offered good holds for hands and feet. Moreover, the nano material of our soft climbing boots and gloves was made not to slip. The rock material wasn't likely to break away, there were no icy passages or overhangs — actually a walk in the park, only the wall lacked any comfortable ledges to rest on. However, a drop from this height would have been lethal.

After consideration of fall likelihood and consequences, we had opted for the rope. We couldn't accept the risk without.

I had reached another spot that looked suitable for a piton. I placed the safety spike, clipped myself into it, and then waited for my partner to close up.

CHAPTER THIRTY-THREE

All clear, no cameras, my partner signaled.

While I climbed the last leg up to her, she kept her eyes on the fortress walls above me, only tossing me an occasional checking glance.

We both didn't expect me to need help — not anymore, at the climbing route's uppermost part, where the rock wall leaned toward the crest. Still, it was part of her task to cover me, so she did it. Mambas on mission are never negligent.

Upon reaching her, I clipped into the second hook and started examining the part of the fortress visible from below. Like Elodie before, I couldn't spot cameras or the movement of guards on the outer wall. That matched our previous findings, our expectations, and our plans — why should anyone bother to guard a non-accessible outer wall? Okay, the access wasn't entirely impossible, which our presence proved, but the effort for such surveillance was disproportionate to the potential risk — any intruder could still be caught upon crossing the wall.

I pulled my backpack forward and began to exchange the gear. I no longer needed the extra pitons and carabiners, hammer and axe. Instead I added the night visor that would only have impeded my climbing, and attached the plasma pistol holsters.

Elodie did the same. Then we checked each other and found ourselves ready.

My watch showed minus six minutes. A bit too early, but within the allowance. A finger wave produced the function menu, a snap triggered the prepared short message.

In position.

CHAPTER THIRTY-FOUR

Nothing stirred on the wall for the next three minutes. Instead, the other five tandem teams' short messages arrived. Six times two Mambas were ready to pay the legal fortress inhabitants a visit and provide their unvoluntary guests with an option to depart.

We all thus had three minutes left to wait for potential guard reactions—if their equipment was good enough to recognize the fractions-of-a-second-long signals, tell them apart from atmospheric noise, and draw the right conclusions.

These three minutes allowed Elodie and me to closely examine the steep slope and the fortress wall and to pick a favorable path to climb.

We had to negotiate this last leg without safety equipment, and we had to be fast. Each grip, each step had to be perfect until we reached the wall crest, so we went through our approach in our minds.

A last glance at my partner, a wink, okay—we were ready.

The pistol holsters were heavily hanging down from my upper legs, and the night visor impaired my view up, but after the first few meters I had adapted to it. When I reached the wall base, I no longer thought about it, and when I climbed the rough-jointed wall, I had no time to worry.

The hardest part was waiting for us when we reached the crest.

Elodie produced a small mirror and held it up over the edge. Were there any guards on this piece of crest? *No,* she signaled.

Okay. I pulled myself up and swung over the parapet, let myself drop to the ground behind, and looked around. Yes, the parapet walk was truly empty. Instead, I spotted two cameras to the left and the right, each quite a distance away from me, observing the inner wall and the tower across the fifth courtyard — exactly our next leg's destination.

These cameras had to go. I waved at Elodie, just arriving next to me, and pointed at the camera to the right. She nodded and hurried away.

The device to the left, maintenance-friendly mounted to the inner railing, was my task. I pulled a thin foil from a belt pouch and held it against the lens.

After a brief moment, I leaned forward and breathed on it. The foil stuck to the lens, and the protruding parts melted away. Miracles of nano technology!

For the next hour, the camera would only show the image sequence it had *seen* up to the moment of breathing-on. Thereafter, the nano foil was used up and would dissolve.

Elodie was already waiting — I gave her a thumbs-up, and both of us swung over the inner railing to climb down to the night-dark fifth courtyard.

CHAPTER THIRTY-FIVE

It was darker inside the wall—the moonlight didn't reach here. Even my night visor had a hard time discovering contours on the evenly cold wall. I had to feel for the individual joints with fingers and toes and soon lost any feeling for my progress.

Then my left foot suddenly and surprisingly encountered opposition—I had arrived on the ground. I carefully placed the second foot next to it and checked for uneven ground before I turned around and scanned the area for threats.

Suspicious noises or movements—negative. Even Elodie was only recognizable because I knew where to find her. Not only did the color of our nano suits disguise us, the suits also shielded our body heat.

Okay, we were inside, and we weren't, because we wouldn't find our target in the fifth courtyard.

The narrow road into the fortress came from the fifth gate to our left and climbed to the sixth gate to our right in eight switchbacks. The *courtyard* was accordingly steep, and the walk to the inner wall somewhat strenuous.

The inner wall's outer face was as easy to climb as the outer wall's—but the crown ended right at the tower. We would need a lot of luck to find the parapet free of guards again.

Our plan wasn't based on luck, though, otherwise our mission would've been busted the moment Elodie scanned the wall with her mirror.

Two, she signaled at me. *Sixteen meters to the left, three meters to the right, standing still.*

The second one was practically standing above her, while I had to climb sixteen meters to the left. How much was that, counted by grooves?

Elodie gave me another signal when I had reached my position, and then confirmed that the two guards hadn't moved away.

It couldn't be helped — we had to cross this wall, and there was no safe way to sneak past these guards. There was only the second option left — eliminating these guards.

Together.

Only a drip of booster for acceleration, and we were jumping over the parapet. My guard didn't even find time for a surprised outcry before my fingertips hit his throat and took his breath for a moment. A slap with the other hand planted a tape on his neck, and then he dropped into my arms — the narcotic was strong and fast.

I glanced to the side — Elodie nodded at me and then placed her victim down in a recovery position. I did the same with my guard.

The path was clear — but had we remained unspotted?

CHAPTER THIRTY-SIX

The parapet was within viewing range of two cameras—
one above the tower door, one on the wall near the gate
between the eighth and ninth courtyard, but the two peacefully sleeping guards had disappeared behind the inner railing curve and were missing in this picture.

Whether we had already been spotted depended on how
attentively someone watched these camera images alone—
were the cameras shown in sequence, and was it this section's
turn again already?

Coordination wasn't necessary. Elodie had spotted the
cameras, too, so we had our targets. Sadly, mine was in the
wrong direction—away from the tower. That couldn't be
helped.

The approach was the same as before—apply foil, wait,
breathe on it. Only I gave the camera a little push first, so that
it no longer captured the supposed piece of wall. The guards
inside might've been wondering whether one of the guards
had leaned against it. In any case, they could no longer recognize that the guards were missing—if they could spot the
black-clad guards on their camera images at all.

Elodie was done with her camera, too.

We met at the entrance from the parapet to the tower, and
I checked the time display at my visor's edge. We had won
another minute against the plan. That didn't mean a thing for
our next steps, but possibly the other teams hadn't reached
their next leg's destination yet. If we encountered resistance,
we'd get all the heat, and the other teams would have easier

going.

This again quite matched my demand. Last time, the others had had their fun alone. Now it was our turn. I had no doubt that Elodie and I could handle anything we'd encounter inside.

I drew my plasma pistols, assumed position before the door, and nodded. Elodie placed her hand on the knob, turned, and slowly pulled the door a finger wide open.

The parapet floor was bathed in warm light. Beyond the gap, I first saw a wall with numerous flatscreens showing different parts of fortress and walls.

Below followed a console, and a lone man was lolling in his swivel chair at that console, the head leaning on one shoulder.

Alerted from the cool breeze, he looked up toward the door and thus toward me. His eyes widened, and then he took a breath and opened his mouth.

Chapter Thirty-Seven

I hit his throat with my outstretched left leg before he could cry out, thus taking away his breath to cry and at the same time preventing him from reaching the alarm button.

My jump's impetus tore him down with his chair while I made a forward roll over him and came down to a crouch— right in front of another guard who could only utter a half-loud "Wha—" before my chop took his air, too.

My searching gaze followed the barrel of the gun in my left—more guards? No—and my right hand caught the tossed-up second plasma pistol that would only have been in the way of my chop.

We safely put these two men out of order with two more narcotic tapes.

Elodie gave me a brief questioning look when I pulled my first victim away from the console, but she immediately nodded when I pointed out the computers under the desk. There were the camera recordings that might give evidence about our approach.

No longer.

Four plasma shots melted the entire gear away.

What next?

The room had three more doors, two in line with the outer wall, and one leading inward. Elodie pointed at the door to the right of the entrance.

Again I positioned myself before the door and let her open it, but behind it was only a small bathroom.

The opposite door led to a break room with refrigerator

and coffee maker—nothing to do for us either.

That left only the inward door. Somewhere beyond the door had to be a stairway up and down, a path to our targets, and more guards. And if everything had gone according to plan, we'd meet two more teams there—Tess and Sabine as well as Justine and Tia—who were supposed to advance through the seventh, eighth and ninth courtyards into the ground floor.

Elodie placed a hand on the handle and looked at me, but I didn't assume position. Instead I fetched the small mirror from my belt. This time, I wanted to see what was waiting for us first, so that we wouldn't give ourselves away and thereby create trouble for the other teams.

At this moment, a shot rang out from somewhere behind the door.

CHAPTER THIRTY-EIGHT

Elodie and I exchanged brief glances, then she drew one gun and pulled the door open with the other hand. More shots rang out from behind, and then we also heard the hiss of plasma shots.

The noises originated from the ground floor. Our mates were in trouble there — but that wasn't what mattered now.

We were beyond the battle zone and still had a chance to reach the targets unmolested. Our priority was clear.

Nobody was standing at our door to keep us from our task. Nevertheless, I paused in surprise — instead of the expected staircase I had stepped on a gently rising ramp nestled to the hollow tower's inner face, helix-like.

Several taut cables were hanging in the hollow center. Elevator or crane? That wasn't important now.

Important was the ramp's railing that shielded us against detection from below. Ducking down, I hurried upward — and stopped right next to it, then gave Elodie a signal, because I had spotted movement four and a half turns further up.

"Go, move!" a resolute voice ordered from there. "And no foolishness!"

Who would order who like that? I glanced at my partner.

Elodie nodded. We had found our target.

Fast now.

A little dose of booster, and I had to run along the outer wall. I jumped across doors in my path. *First turn done.*

The rush of air tore at my hair. It no longer mattered that the sound of air gave us away. *Second turn.*

More shots rang out from below. The defenders couldn't get out through the plasma barrage, but our teams couldn't get in either. *Third turn.*

A door clapped shut, only one turn above us. I held the guns forward and aimed at the height where I knew the door hinged — the hinges of the doors we already had passed had all been placed ramp-upward.

The door came into view. I shot twice, thus eliminating the hinges, pushed myself inward, bounced back from the railing and broke through the door's remains. I rolled off inside, looked at surprised faces and at several machine pistol barrels leveling toward me.

Chapter Thirty-nine

Four men in black leather with machine pistols, standing. Two men and one woman, sitting and unarmed — the situation assessment wasn't hard.

Two targets, two shots, two opponents less.

I'd been too late for the other two, but I could rely on Elodie.

The guards had never had a chance — at least not after they had assembled in one room with our targets. We didn't have time for sleep tapes here.

I'd deal with my conscience later. Only the mission counted now.

I straightened myself, raised my plasma pistol barrels to the ceiling and smiled at the three researchers. "Filipa Lopes, Gustave Aubertin, Song Qin Chao? I am Monique, this is my partner Elodie, and I'm conveying an invitation from Johanna Meier, also known as Velvet, for a visit of the new Dragon University. As an alternative, I'm authorized to take you to a place of your choice. I only must advise you against staying in this fortress."

Elodie stood next to the doorframe and peeked out. I tapped the communicator with one spread-out finger and sent one of the predefined signals. The others had to know we had found the three target persons. Thus the mission had entered the third phase — getting them out safely.

The researchers' gazes met. The Asian eyeballed the dead, and then he bowed forward. "I was tempted to say you've got no chance to get out of here alive — and neither do we. Our guards have very clearly told us what they'd do to us in case of an escape attempt." He pointed at his companions in misfortune. "We're very fond of our lives. But the task we're supposed to complete here very much displeases us, and we've seen what you just did. Your reflexes are unusually fast. Supernatural. Or am I wrong?"

"No," I admitted. "We're doped."

He showed a thin-lipped smile. "I can't tell if that will suffice against our guards. The *Dragon Claws* are extraordinarily fast, too. But you could have a chance, and I'm willing to bet on that chance. What about you?"

Chao looked to the side. Filipa and Gustave nodded.

"Who are the *Dragon Claws?*" I asked.

Chao rose. "Three men with the order to prevent our escape. The same applies to all others here, too, but these three were sent from *the top,* whatever that means. They're better than the others, from some special unit. Without doubt people one should beware of."

Elodie looked at me. "Like us."

I nodded. "There could be others." Then I turned to the three researchers. "Our people are keeping the guards on the ground floor busy. If we stay close to the wall, crouch, and stay quiet, we can escape across the parapet. I'll go ahead, Elodie has our backs. Ready?"

"As ready as one can be," Chao agreed, and his companions nodded.

"Good. From now on, no talk." I crouched, pushed my way past Elodie, and began the descent.

Our way down would take longer and we wouldn't have trouble with centrifugal forces. The researchers couldn't keep up with our speed, and I needed not to advance more than a quarter turn ahead.

Still, single shots rang out from below. Had they come to terms with the standoff? Or was Tess preparing a new move?

The only warning was a sudden swelling hiss. Then a man in a skintight black suit appeared before me, a short, crooked blade in each hand, and he was ragingly *fast.*

CHAPTER FORTY

B*ooster!*
Only with *accelerated* reflexes did I manage the jump out of his blades' reach—for one moment I was balancing on the ramp's railing, but he had already stopped, turned to me, slashed at me again.

His sabers hacked deep nicks into the concrete railing while I was landing on the ramp below, trying to swing my pistols in his direction. I didn't find time to consider why he was using blades instead of firearms.

He jumped at me before I could pull the trigger, and again, only a bold jump to the side could save me—but this time he had expected it and drew the blade in his left hand across my left lower leg.

The pressure on my leg gave me a feel for his tremendous power. Without doubt, the cut would have completely severed my leg if my nano suit's material hadn't protected me, but the steel felt dull on it.

So he only pushed my leg aside, made me fight for my balance, and his second blade was already coming for me.

I let myself fall backward into the open shaft, then gave myself another impulse with the rear leg that carried me into the shaft's center. One pistol clicked into its holster.

I needed that hand to grab one of the cables in the center.

While I was swinging around it, I fired a salvo toward the ground floor. It didn't matter what I hit—I couldn't afford to lose track of my opponent who was just climbing the railing to follow me! It only mattered to make the stay down there very, very uncomfortable and thus give our reinforcements a chance to enter the tower and support us.

Some machine pistol salvos followed the plasma hits' rising heat—likewise poorly aimed and yet another good reason not to linger at the cable, aside from my primary opponent, who jumped at me with his two blades.

That way, he jumped into the machine pistol salvos while I had already swung around the cable and flown back over the railing—bad luck for him! Neither of the bullets had been meant for him, but now he was in the wrong place at the wrong time, and all his speed didn't help him there. He caught numerous hits, yelled in fury—his first statement—and then hit the cable.

Blood sprayed from many wounds, and the firing from below fell silent.

From the railing I could see the understanding dawn on him that he'd done something very foolish. Not just due to the hail of lead he had jumped into—but because he now, hanging from the cable with injured, weakened arms, had no chance to profit from his enhancement.

My first plasma round hit him right in the chest, the second in the head, and relieved him from his pain. His grip loosened, and he fell.

Before those below could overcome their surprise, I took cover behind the railing. A hot feeling in my right butt cheek told me that at least one bullet had grazed me, and I didn't need more of those.

Irrelevant.

Relevant was only one question I pondered while hurrying toward Elodie and our protégés—where were the two other *Dragon Claws?*

CHAPTER FORTY-ONE

A furious roar from the ground floor, following the thunk of a body, at least partially answered this question.

The source of this bestial sound started moving *fast* around the tower axis and up without falling silent.

"Take them to cover," I told Elodie. "I'll stop him."

She only had time for a brief sad glance, and then she nodded and signaled the researchers to retreat into a room farther up the ramp.

The roar was only one turn away.

Thoughtfully, I regarded the ramp floor before me, as far as I could see around the railing's bend — then I placed several well-calculated plasma shots and waited.

My opponent might have been angry, unrestrained, and *fast* — but he wasn't so foolish as to step on a red-hot glowing concrete surface. He jumped across.

The jump was fast, too, but he was in the air long enough — and thus not able to change course — so that I could score one safe hit each.

Or almost safe. He recognized the trap, tossed himself around in mid-air, and my plasma shots hit his right hip and left shoulder only.

The plasma hissed on his flesh, and the pitch of his roar changed. That hurt, very certainly, and the wounds would impede him.

I held my hands to my hips — click, click, the pistols attached to their holsters — and danced to the right when my opponent landed on his feet before me and dashed at me with swirling blades right away.

His injured right hip didn't play along when he tried to follow my move, and his left arm wouldn't cooperate.

My battering blow against his left hand sadly didn't yield the desired effect, either—I didn't manage to knock the weapon out of his hand.

In exchange, his second blade came for my arm. In turn, I could easily block that.

He drew his returning left blade along my chest—again, in vain.

He made one step back, the blades held out threateningly, and slightly shook his head. He had three assumed advantages—he was a strong man, he had his enhancement, and his two blades.

I was a strong and most of all very swift woman, I was enhanced as well, and his blades couldn't penetrate my suit. Moreover, I was drilled to fight for my life. Was he, too? Plus he was severely injured with his burned hip and shoulder. The facts favored me—or not?

He grinned. With growing horror I had to watch his shoulder wound slowly close. What kind of opponent was this?

CHAPTER FORTY-TWO

This was the kind of opponent you'd better avoid, but this option wasn't available to me—I couldn't allow him to reach Elodie and our protégés.

I had no time to gamble for either. That left only one option—attack.

That I did. Step forward, beat blades aside, then a strike at the throat . . . that was the plan. The plan didn't work, though, because my opponent didn't let his arms get beaten aside—he was too strong.

Instead, I was within his reach, now, and he pushed his arms inward to stab me with his long blades.

The nano fabric over my tummy hardened to distribute the pressure, and of course the tip didn't penetrate, but the double strike hurt anyway.

Okay, his arms didn't give? Then I could use them as support and haul myself up and over him *fast*.

Likewise fast he turned around and came for me before I had entirely come down. *Merde!*

So I had to extend my dash forward—but there was the heated ramp area, so I'd have to jump far, and for the duration of the jump my movement would be calculable. *No, thanks!*

I jumped sideways against the outer wall, pushed myself away from there and over the railing, only grabbing it at the last moment to reroute myself to the ramp below. That way I had left his view and his range—and was no longer between him and Elodie.

This couldn't remain like that, so I ran—quietly!—a quarter

turn up the ramp, jumped on the railing and catapulted myself forcefully upward. I had to jump away from the ramp, so the next part was crucial — I had to hook one foot into the next level's lower edge to initiate a turn, then grab the railing and support the outward turn, and finally come down on my legs firmly enough to react to the already upcoming man again. It was no surprise that I could only just so escape an unsighted shot from the ground floor . . .

My opponent approached with a deep red face. He radiated heat like a small oven.

I ducked to the side under his stab, clasped one foot with my legs and jerked, thus bringing my opponent down. That was the beauty in judo — his superior power didn't help him against that.

Of course, he tried to jump up again immediately.

I was a bit faster, because I had significantly less mass to move, and I levered him down once again. The brief body contact required made me reconsider my idea of applying a stranglehold — he was just much too hot!

He seemed to give up his attempt to get on his feet again, and instead kicked at me. I dodged and reached for a gun — as long as he was down, I had a chance.

He saw the same — or had he planned this? He catapulted his entire body up and kicked me — he hit me in the chest, took my breath away and shoved me down the ramp. The plasma pistol flew away, landing many meters behind me.

And he came after me, his face distorted with fury, meanwhile so hot that the air around him was hazy!

He didn't come *fast*. He saw me fighting for my breath. *Damn, girl, get up! Move as long as you can!* Only — I no longer could. I felt a sting in my chest — were my ribs broken?

It took me an effort to wrap my fingers around the remaining pistol's grip. My opponent saw it and showed an evil grin. We both knew I wouldn't be fast enough.

The blades in his hand showed a reddish glow, heated up by his radiation. I wouldn't have been surprised if he had grown horns on his head and hid a hoof in his boot.

Come closer. Slowly. Perhaps your heat will make my plasma magazine burn through. Then I can at least take you with me.

Instead he reached for my neck *fast*. I felt the pressure and knew that my nano suit couldn't protect me against his grip.

Nor could I hope for a merciful broken neck. His intention was to slowly strangle me—if my neck wouldn't burn away before that, I recognized with the last remainders of mental clarity.

Chapter Forty-Three

His head burst, glowing fragments spraying in all directions. Right away a gleaming ball burned into his chest — only my visor saved me from turning temporarily blind.

"What did I teach you?" Tess ranted over my head and tossed my opponent's dead body aside. "Always stay in motion, never let yourself be nailed down!"

She went on one knee at my side and leaned over me. She cautiously moved my visor up with both hands. "Are you okay?"

I tried to say something, but found no breath. Instead I closed my eyes twice.

"No. All right. I'll have a look."

A gentle finger press let my nano suit open at the neck. By moving two fingers right and left around my neck, then up my chin, and across my chest to the navel, she expanded the opening.

Her first comment was a sharp hiss.

"Sabine, healing tape!"

A moment later, I felt a cooling touch at my neck.

"Burns and bruises — no wonder you can't talk. That'll be better soon."

I heard steps — first the quiet whisper of Justine's and Tia's feet, clearly not determined to sneak, thereafter the steps of the three researchers, and last, Elodie's. My partner stopped and also went on her knees at my side, took my hand and squeezed it.

"What happened?" asked Tess.

"I didn't see anything. After Monique shot the first berserker, the second stormed up roaring, and Monique sent us to the side room."

I felt the breathing becoming easier.

"What—three?" I whispered.

"Quiet." Our leader placed another tape on my chest. "You've got quite a bruise there, too. Once I've treated that, we must go. Lucy and Laura took out the third berserker, and that was a hard piece of work. Both have taken some. You've got away nice."

I didn't feel like that.

"Ribs—broken," I whispered.

"But—" Elodie began.

"Quiet. Sabine, give me an energy pack. Elodie, we won't leave Monique behind, but we must go. The nanos will prevent the worst. We only have to wrap Monique well and carry her carefully. Monique, you'll hold out, won't you?"

"Sure." I wasn't entirely clear about that. If I had known what *carry carefully* meant—but that came later.

CHAPTER FORTY-FOUR

Chao brought me a glass of red sparkling wine and then sat down in the rattan chair next to me.

"Nanette told me," he explained.

Then he remained silent, waited until I had taken a sip.

"Thank you."

"I must thank you," he objected.

"What for?"

"You risked your life for us. Does it still hurt?"

"No. The pain fades soon, only the memory lingers longer." And the stay in the nano healing tank wasn't pleasant, but helped. The worst had been the transport to the landing place where Zoé had collected us. The girls had made every effort not to shake me, but the ribs had protested with every step anyway.

"I don't know at all how we can make good for that."

"You don't have to." He wasn't happy with that reply, I noticed. "With what I've done, I've paid a little share of my debt with Jo."

Chao smiled. "I see. Then we should work on our debt for Johanna."

"You owe Jo nothing either. We only contributed to correcting a wrong. You're free, that was the mission objective." I drank a larger sip and enjoyed the intense berry flavor.

"I can't ignore what you're doing here."

I shrugged. "Many here feel the same."

He pointed at the counter. "Like Nanette?"

"Yes. Like Nanette."

"What did Jo do for her?"

"Nothing."

"Nothing?" Chao glanced at Nanette again.

"Well, not much. Nanette was a waitress in southern France. Jo brought her together with François. François works for Jo—and so Nanette came with him."

"She's very dedicated."

"Indeed." I had to smile, too.

"Where does that come from?"

"What we're doing here is important. That's our motivation."

"The fight against injustice?"

"The fight for mankind's survival, Chao. Preparations against the Jellies' second wave. That's what we're working for."

"And that's what you need us for."

That couldn't be denied. "You could help. If you like."

"If we like. You like?"

"That's why I'm still here. I could leave if I wanted—but I don't want to."

"Perhaps later?"

"Perhaps. Unlikely. You've seen what we're working on?" I waved toward the pinboard.

"The topics? Impressive."

"I could be among the first to set foot on a distant planet."

He sat up straight. "Where's that written?"

"Many of the cards show topics related to it."

"Hum. I might have to take another closer look."

"I warn you. It might be that you can't get away from it."

Chao chuckled. "That's how it works?"

"That's how it works."

"So you were quite confident we would stay."

I smiled and nodded. "If we hadn't had to free you first, you'd have come long ago."

INTERLUDE

CHAPTER FORTY-FIVE

Nanette watched me heaving the heavy box onto the upper board with a worried face.

"Doesn't that hurt?" she asked.

"No."

In fact I still felt a slight drag in my leg and a pressure in the chest when making such efforts. From my point of view, that didn't count as real pain.

We had a machine somewhere for the transport of such provisions, but whenever Nanette had something heavy to lift, an armor suit bearer or one of us enhanced team members was near to help.

I followed her to the bar. On my way I fetched a tea towel — I had spotted some newly washed glasses before which hadn't been cleared away yet. Unloading and loading of Freddie's yacht came always first because the jetty access could only be navigated at high tide. The heavy box had been the last, though.

Nanette had to tend to her guests again — a small group of researchers had gathered in one corner of the center to discuss a problem with the precise synchronization of control quark emitters for larger missiles. Luckily I didn't have to rack my brain on such topics.

Instead I reflected on the fortress berserkers while toweling, on the *Dragon Claws,* as they called themselves according to Chao. They were significantly faster than ordinary humans, also with fast reactions, stronger, able to heal themselves, obviously not very sensitive to pain — or in any case they showed little reaction to severe hits—and at least my second opponent had been very uncontrolled, like a poorly adjusted Mamba before Johanna's treatment.

The intense unfolding heat didn't fit into the picture. My opponent had practically fried himself, but that seemingly hadn't harmed him much. Was that typical?

My first fast opponent hadn't survived long enough to run hot. But he hadn't been as furious, either. He reminded me of another surprisingly fast antagonist in a lodge in the Canadian Rockies . . .

"*Merde!*"

"*Quoi?*" Nanette returned, but I was already on my way.

The jetty looked deserted—Freddie's yacht was already heading for the mainland, so there was nothing to do here.

"*Merde!*" I cursed again.

The air near the jetty's landward end flickered, and one of our armor suits became visible.

"Monique, what's up?"

"Orry, did you see Tess or Sabine?"

"Mmm—last time yesterday. They went to the mainland with Freddie."

I slapped my forehead. "Yes, sure. Shielding. I forgot—I'm not scheduled again yet. One week's rest, Peter said. Do you know where Arko is?"

"He's holding a seminar about xeno-biology, I guess. Something about the adaptation to living conditions on foreign planets."

"What does he know about it?"

"His kind isn't from here, right?"

I only nodded. Yes, you could easily forget or deny this fact, like the fact that Dragons, even in human shape, retained the memories of several generations of their ancestors.

All right. If he was busy, I had to be patient. Then I might as well return to toweling glasses.

CHAPTER FORTY-SIX

I am a Mamba. I am strong and confident. I'm an equal member of Jo's team. I don't have to hide.

Nevertheless, I felt small and stupid in Achrotzyber's presence. He was simply so — present. Masculine and dominant. Smart. And he was looking so fucking good!

"How are you?" he began. "Can I do something for you?"

"I'm fine. My injuries are healed." I couldn't hold his gaze and watched the treetops above us instead. How did Jo always word it? "I arrived at a different extrapolation."

"With regard to what?"

"During the last mission, we met three men with special abilities."

"I have heard about that. They were similarly enhanced to you."

"It seems like that — aside from the improved self-healing and the unusual heat radiation."

"I have not heard about that."

Damn, how does he manage to stand there like a statue? Not even the sun seems to blind him!

"Didn't Tess tell you anything?"

"No. She kept it short. She was — worried about you. She wanted to get back to the tank soon."

"*Merde.*"

Now he looked irritated.

"A French expletive," I explained. "I'm unhappy. You're not sufficiently briefed." Had I been able to tell Tess everything? With Arko I could now correct this shortcoming, and I tried to list every detail of my fights with the two *Dragon Claws*. "Moreover, I remembered we might have encountered such an opponent before." I reported my Canadian encounter again. "The guy was unusually fast, too. Only he wasn't quite as good. Yes, and then I considered why he was there at all — in any case, not as a guard. Should Peter do something with him?"

"Go on."

"What?"

"About your different extrapolation."

"Oh. Right. Yes. Well — there must be an organization somewhere training such modified persons. If they appear in Canada and China, it's a worldwide organization. I deduce that our opponents by and by recover from the decapitation — from the Cartel headquarters elimination — and are beginning to pull their strings anew. Moreover, if they can afford to send out such enhanced men in groups, they might have more of them? There must be a training center somewhere. Is it okay to wait for them to deploy an army of such men and set them upon us to take their researchers back? I mean, what we can do, they can do, too. Are we currently able to repel such an attack? Possibly with taking hostages, which impedes us much worse than those people?"

The big Dragon man nodded. "That is an interesting extrapolation."

"And they know where they'll have to look for us."

"Of course. We must prepare. Please summon your partners who are on the island. I will talk with Kenneth and Ron. We will meet at Nanette's place."

CHAPTER FORTY-SEVEN

A side from Elodie, I found only Zoé, Gwen and Avril on the Island. The latter two had just returned from their shielding duty on the mainland.

Arko brought the suit bearer Cody in addition to Kenneth and Ron—only now without his suit, as he was off duty.

"Monique has to report important observations to you," the Dragon began without transition. "Monique, please tell them about your mission's relevant parts again."

Under Arko's critical gaze, I recapped my solo fights during the Canadian and Chinese missions. Only the facts, Tess always demanded, and when a Dragon was listening, I had to get my story straight—my own interpretations and conclusions didn't belong in my narration. Instead, I had to mention all the little details that had influenced my assessment.

In the end, the Dragon man nodded. "Elodie, please add your observations now."

My partner nodded, too. "Canada first? Okay—as Monique already said, we had gone separate ways. I was searching the upper floor when I heard shots from below—from a pistol, so probably not Monique's. I got ready to encounter alarmed and armed persons on my floor as well—when a man came from one room and trained a pistol in my direction. I quickly took cover in the next door frame so that he missed me, and returned fire. I had aimed well and should have hit him. His reaction came very fast—he had already broken through another door. Where the doors were actually too robust to break so easily."

"How fast was he?" Arko asked.

"I saw him too briefly to safely tell that. He appeared very fast in reaction to me, but as he had stopped in the corridor, I couldn't tell anything about his speed."

"Thank you. What did you notice during the recent mission?"

"The first opponent—I was behind the three researchers, about one third of the ramp circumference behind, and had a good view of everything that happened above the railing. The man was positively as fast as we can only be with booster, and he was armed with two sabers. He hacked a deep nick into the concrete railing with a single strike—neither of us could do that, not even with our enhancement." Elodie illustrated the further sequence of combat. "Meanwhile I moved in front of the researchers so I could protect them, and drew my weapons—but the duel was moving back and forth too fast for a safe shot, and then Monique jumped into the shaft, he followed, and when Monique was back on the ramp and shot, I held my fire to not give away my presence." She nodded at me. "Moni got along well. Therefore, I wasn't worried to leave her alone with the next opponent. I've only noted his roar, and that noise approached us truly *fast*."

"And afterward?"

"Well—I was mainly looking after Monique. Well, yes—I'd seen the blades, too, and I thought, better not step on them, they must be darn hot."

"From a plasma hit?" Ron asked.

"No, surely not. Too evenly and not melted."

"What kind of people are they?" Kenneth asked. "A new kind of Mambas?"

"No," Arko firmly disagreed. "No ordinary or enhanced human body can stand such heat over the duration of a battle. The body material would burn."

"What are they, then?"

"A kind of Dragon."

CHAPTER FORTY-EIGHT

The shock sat deeply with the others. I could hardly grasp it either.

"I have fought *two* Dragons?"

Arko looked at me. "So it seems, although neither of them was as capable as a grown-up Dragon in human shape could be. We do not have enough data to prove this hypothesis though."

"What do we call them, then? Berserkers?"

"Dragonlings," Elodie proposed.

Kenneth cleared his throat. "What chances would we have to repel an attack of several such Dragonlings? Okay, Monique proved she can prevail against such an opponent, if he isn't prepared for a Mamba. But where do you stand in battle, Ron?"

Our armor suit leader glanced at his side. "Cody, perhaps you could say something?"

"You know how it is, Ron. We regularly exercise against each other, gals against blokes. The result is entirely open — we're armored, invisible and well-armed, and can't be defeated with bare hands, but if you put a plasma pistol into a Mamba's hand, she can take out two or three of us. If she shows herself too early, she's done with. A hit from the linear cannon would be as final. Overall, it's a tie." He spread his hands. "If these Dragonlings can survive our hits and fight on after we unveil our location, I don't know how we could stop them. It probably all depends on whether they can sneak as well as Mambas."

"I don't think I could have taken one of them out without a gun," I added. "My opponent was damn strong — I wouldn't have wanted to try a neck lever. With a gun — well, he dodged me several times. You must find a good moment to score. During a jump, for example."

"Or fire a crossed salvo that covers it all. Steel thunderstorm." Cody shrugged. "Of course, that only works if the firing range is otherwise free."

"Iron storm," Ron corrected and gave Arko an apologetic glance. "Part of the Dragon defense drill."

"Naturally." The Dragon man focused on me. "Monique advised me that our means of defense do not suffice. She also advised me that we do not know yet where these Dragonlings were trained."

The men looked aghast back and forth between him and me.

"There could be more," I confirmed.

Kenneth nodded. "Of course. The four were hardly born where we met them. Can you even say *born,* or would it better be *made?*"

"Does that matter?" Ron asked.

"Well — the natural way is a limiting factor." Kenneth shrugged apologetically. "Not just time-wise."

Elodie shook her head. "We've got too little data. We don't know how they do it and we don't know where they do it. We don't even know how long they've been doing it. How old did these people look? Thirtyish?"

"That would give a clue." Kenneth leaned forward. "Then they were born sometime before the Invasion."

I raised a concern. "If our opponents were the first of their kind."

"That is not true."

All gazes turned to Arko.

"My *memory* contains further encounters. The Imperatrix

Zoe Lionheart had two such encounters. That was in April 2008 in Germany and in May 2008 in Egypt. Her opponent was about eighteen years old back then."

CHAPTER FORTY-NINE

The questions weren't painted on my face alone.

"So you know about that already," Kenneth noted, looking at Arko.

"I possess this information," Arko corrected. "I was not aware of it, though. It requires an outside cue or an all-encompassing search to retrieve such *memories.*"

"All right. Even Dragons cannot think of everything at the same time. Only we'll have to reassess the threat potential for the worse situation, won't we?"

Zoé cleared her throat. "Your memory doesn't contain information on these people's origin, does it? We know what they look like, and what they call themselves, but we don't know at all how, when, and why they show up. What have they got to do with the remnants of the Cartel? How do their appearances back then and now relate? Can we collect some of that?"

"Good idea." Elodie squinted. "There are two things that set our missions in Canada and China apart from the others— the Canada location was designed for outside visits, and in China, three locations were joined. Both targets belong to a supranational organization we don't know yet."

"And Russia?" I asked. "The station there definitely belonged to a *Syndicate.*" I tried to recap the sequence of events there and uttered a juicy curse.

"What?" my partner asked.

"The giant. Do you remember? Five guys Tess had to wheedle into freeing the path to the G corridor. One appeared nervous, almost like feverish."

"And you mean—"

"I mean nothing. The build matches—as athletic as the *Dragon Claws*. The nervousness matches a poorly adjusted Mamba, just like with the others. On top comes the fever—I remember he appeared hot to me. It's quite possible he's one of them. We must factor that in."

"It would fit." Elodie focused on the Dragon man. "Three locations with supranational connections, three times reinforcement of the guard staff with such a Dragonling—no, I correct myself, in Canada he was no guard but a patient. We should ask Peter about that. What I'm driving at, though, according to Zoé's proposal—our unknown antagonists are ready to send out their creations to the world, but perhaps only in a controlled environment so far."

"We can't tell that," Kenneth objected. "You encounter these people only there because you're going only there. Until now we didn't know what to look for, so there are no independent sightings yet. Our people could have encountered such a guy umpteen times without noticing."

"And so we wouldn't even know if they're already assembling in Gladstone." Ron gave Cody a gloomy glance. "We need immediate measures before talking about strategy. Arko, I must brief my men. Now."

Kenneth nodded. "We must tell Tess and the others, and I should talk with some people in Canberra soon."

"Should Elodie and I have a look around on the mainland?" I asked.

"No," Arko immediately decided. "Monique, you are the only one with combat experience against the Dragonlings. You will go with Ron and explain what the men should watch out for. Zoé, you will take Kenneth to the mainland, inform Tess, and then fly him to Canberra." He looked at Kenneth, who nodded in surprise, and then at my partner. "Elodie will tell the researchers and thereafter ask Peter about the Canadian Dragonling."

"And you?" my partner asked Arko.

"I will transform myself to protect the Island."

CHAPTER FIFTY

Twelve pairs of eyes were focused on me. Twelve healthy, strong and heterosexual men gave me their entire professional attention, and none of them looked at my bare tits. That made me, truth be told, somewhat nervous.

They were sitting before me in the sand in a quarter circle, some cross-legged, presenting me with their privates, and I had no eye for those. I pushed my bare foot back and forth in the sand, looked each of them in the eye in sequence, pondered.

It had been a brief but delicate consideration—should I deal with our suit bearers in two sittings in turn, so that one group could continue to protect us, or all together? All together, Arko had decided—the sooner they knew, the sooner they were ready for the worst possible case.

How should I start? No, I won't turn to Ron for help now.

"Okay. I don't know how much Cody already told you. We met a new opponent during the last mission, three men of a company that calls itself *Dragon Claws*. I fought two of them in sequence. I survived the first fight because I was good, and the second because I got help in time—and I only defeated the first opponent because I was lucky and had a plasma pistol."

I looked into partially surprised, partially terrified faces. I had fought most of these men before, so they knew how good I was.

"These men wore no protective suits. They were physically better, like me—better than me. I'm fast, these men are, too. But moreover, they are as strong as you with your amplifiers, they can ignore pain, and they heal a grazing shot within moments. Arko calls them *Dragonlings.*"

Perhaps I should have prepared a cheat sheet in advance on what to tell them and in what order.

Nonsense. When a Mamba goes into fight, there's no cheat sheet either, and the planned order is Jelly goo in an instant upon enemy contact.

It has to work without one.

"The name comes from an assumed combination of human and Dragon genes. I've so-to-speak fought two half-dragons. Let's get to the good news — they can be hurt by ordinary machine pistols, and they die when you burn their head or chest away with a plasma gun. They can be tricked, and my impression is that they act less smart when they're angry."

"I think you should report your duels once again now," Cody proposed. I gave him a grateful smile.

"Okay. I'll start with the last mission. There I met two of these Dragonlings, luckily only one by one. We already had freed our protégés . . ."

"I must probably have surprised him with my immediate shot — he didn't expect me to be *fast.* Conversely, I didn't understand back then that there was something unusual about my opponent. I only thought he was good. Only with the experience from China did I judge the Canadian mission differently."

"Ugly situation," Orry commented and gazed at Cody. "But it doesn't seem to be an unsolvable problem, eh?"

"If you know about it, no. If some of those guys had caught us on the wrong foot . . ."

"Yes. I see what you mean." Orry nodded at me. "Okay. What else?"

"Uh, what else?" I had reported it all!

"You fought these people, and you know what we can do. What do we need to do to take out such a guy?"

"Ah." This question was clear to me. "Shoot to kill. Everything else is too uncertain. Assume you only get one shot and aren't invisible to these guys thereafter. Assume—if they could see you, they've already seen you, and only pretend to be innocent. Assume they can hear or smell each of your moves."

The men didn't like my words, but they listened. "Assume these people can handle pistols and rifles—and most of all, blades. Assume your armor won't protect you when it comes to close combat, so don't let it get that far, if you don't outnumber them at least five to one."

"Why five to one?"

"One as bait plus one per limb to tie him down. Then I expect the bait to survive." I shrugged. "Maybe I overestimate the threat. I know you're good, but I don't know how good the Dragonlings can be. I'd wish you won't have to reach your own assessment soon—but we've met here for this possibility, haven't we?"

I heard the sand crunch behind me, and then Scrubby jumped into my field of vision.

Ron stepped to my side. "Thanks, Monique, for your precise descriptions and your assessment. I'd like to ask you to stay while we're considering first strategies. Your insights are valuable for us."

"Oh, sure."

"Thanks. Guys, we need plans. Think about it for a moment, then I want to hear first proposals."

CHAPTER FIFTY-ONE

The tapping of bare feet on the jetty's hard wood slowly came closer, but didn't distract me from watching the ray as it gently swam along below me. I resisted the temptation to glide into the water and follow it — the fishes around our island weren't that trusting.

"May I?" Reginald asked.

"Sure."

Our head of research sat down and let his legs dangle next to mine. He remained silent for a while and let his gaze wander across the sea.

"Idyllic," he finally stated.

The ray disappeared between the corals. In his place, a small shark approached.

"It's easier for the fishes," Reginald commented. "They don't care about distant problems."

"You didn't come to talk about fishes."

"No."

"But?"

"How good are these Dragonlings?"

"How good? In what way?"

"In fighting."

"I don't know."

"I don't understand. You fought them."

"Yes. I can tell you they're fast and strong. No, more precisely — three of them were fast. Two were strong as well. There's one more Lucy took out, who I can't judge. All four could fight, but *good*? They didn't have to be good, and in any

133

case they weren't good enough, as they're dead now."

"Hm."

"My three all made the same mistake. They stood still long enough to be shot down."

"So. I had hoped you could judge how dangerous they are."

"That's a different question. They are very dangerous. They're dangerous because they can take a lot and deal out a lot more. They're dangerous because we know so little about them. They can surprise us."

"Yes, I know. Ron said about the same."

"We don't even know how many there are."

"Or where they come from."

"Exactly. And if we knew —"

"You'd go and take them out," Reginald ended my sentence.

"We couldn't do anything anyway," I corrected him.

"No? But why?"

"We're not killer commandos, Reg. Freeing kidnapped victims is one thing. Kidnapping is illegal."

"Jo even got an okay for your missions. We're at war, and we need the researchers. If someone protested, she'd take the heat. If I remember right, Rashid authorized it as *strategically necessary procurement.*"

I gave him an astonished glance.

Reginald grinned. "It's actually too late for that, but I've seen a note according to which all accredited Dragon technology researchers, should they desire so, can become Velvet Island citizens, tax free, and thus are under the Dragon empress's protection. Rashid plans to have something like this ratified by the UNO."

"What for?"

"*Under the Dragon empress's protection* means that Jo may legally take care of anyone protected anywhere in the world, or send out her delegates to this purpose. You."

"Us?"

He leaned back and focused on me. "Of course you. Who else? She doesn't have enough Dragons for such missions — oh, don't give me that worried look, of course there are no publications about you. But she can't give rein to you without clear legal foundation — if worst comes to worst, you must be covered."

"She must be covered. I thought the less she knows about us, the better it would be for her."

"So that everything's on your bill? Do you know Jo so little?" He put a hand on my shoulder. "Pardon me. No, I understand. You want to protect Jo, just like she wants to protect you."

His touch felt good, reminded me that I hadn't cuddled with a man for a while. With a shrug, I shook off that thought and his hand.

"It doesn't matter anymore. We've completed the list. The fortress was the last mission."

"And what about the Dragonling origin?"

"Nothing. There are none protected, so we don't have any business there."

"No." He appeared disappointed and relieved at the same time, sat up straight, and stared out on the ocean.

"We must wait until they come to us."

"That's not good." He leaned back. "That's not good at all."

"You don't have to worry about that."

"No. I'm worried anyway. I'm always worried. Don't get me wrong now — you're all good friends."

"Tess."

"Yes, she means a lot to me. Like Jo. And both are always at the forefront, and are almost searching for danger." Again he looked at me. "There's hardly a night I can sleep in peace. Even when they're both here, I'm worried what risk they're daring next." He slapped his upper legs. "It won't get better by knowing we're all marked targets. We must deal with the problem. I'll talk with Kenneth."

Then he rose and left, left me alone with my thoughts and my fishes.

CHAPTER FIFTY-TWO

The last firm fin-strokes took me to the small footbridge beneath the jetty. There, I pulled myself up at the ladder, then took the hand my partner held out for me, and let myself be pulled out of the water.

I removed the diving goggles with my free hand, spat out the snorkel mouthpiece, and smiled at Elodie.

"You're catching up." She gave me a towel and took my snorkel and goggles. "If you go on like this, my lead will be gone."

I rubbed my face and hair. "You're getting faster, too."

"Only a little." She took the towel and began to dry me systematically.

I straightened and stretched, bent back and forth, so that she could reach everywhere. *Oooh, that's good!* "Mmmm."

Elodie knew exactly what I liked, and she seemed to be in the mood, too. She helped me out of the fins and then felt her way up. I extended one leg to the side and placed the foot on the railing of the stairs up to the jetty. I felt my outer labia separate.

My partner took her time, wiping off the salty ocean water on my skin before she tossed the towel away and stroked my thighs' sensitive skin with her fingertips.

She moved behind me and began to caress me with one hand inward from the hipbones while the other hand's fingers massaged my buttocks. I pushed my foot on the railing higher, spread my legs even more, and enjoyed the airy feel in my crotch. Moreover, this position allowed me to stretch my strained leg muscles, haha.

Elodie knew what I needed now. One hand approached my clitoris, the other stroked down my butt crack, found my anus, and one finger found its way inside.

Deeper, I thought, while she went around my pink button and explored how wet I already was.

She didn't get distracted even when footsteps sounded on the jetty. Just the opposite, she now felt encouraged to help me to a quicker and more intense orgasm.

I only regretted that I couldn't return the favor right away. But when I took my leg from the railing and eased it, the new-comer was already kicking his heels.

"What's up, Orry?" Elodie asked.

"We've got a lead."

CHAPTER FIFTY-THREE: ARIA PARLANTE INFURIATA

Tess, Sabine, and Kenneth were already waiting for us in the community center.

"You were away?" our team leader asked.

"Swimming exercise," I explained. "Once around reef, only twenty-two kilometers. Doing it in five hours is good, isn't it?"

"I admit I can't judge that time."

"Twenty-five kilometers in about five and a half hours are the official world record," Elodie helped out. "I don't know it precisely either."

"All right. Well, you won't need swimming exercise for a while."

Elodie shrugged. "Running exercises around the island are boring. You're around too quickly."

Tess briefly grinned, and then made a serious face again. "Orry told you we got a lead?"

She waited for our brief nods and went on, "Okay. We're going into the mountains. From the indications our researchers picked up and from the German intelligence service's findings, we came across a mountain farm in Switzerland. Further research showed us that this region is shielded quite thoroughly—mountain hikers' access is blocked systematically. That's conspicuous, so we decided to have a look."

Elodie nodded.

I hesitated for a moment, which didn't escape Tess.

139

"Did you notice something?"

"No, not exactly," I admitted. "I've just been already musing for days what legitimation we can rely on here. After all, we know nothing about hostages or kidnapping victims to free."

She nodded. "You've got a point there. We don't expect to find kidnapped people there—surely no Dragon technology experts. That legitimation option isn't available. Kenneth?"

"The Australian Department of Foreign Affairs contacted the Swiss. That was part of the research Tess mentioned, and there was some messaging back and forth. Firstly, the Swiss were slightly indignant about our snooping, but we could quickly clarify that we had only made connections between witness statements and files, and that we didn't violate their territory. Secondly, they didn't appreciate not having heard about this facility at all, and third, they didn't like someone blocking off an area which that someone doesn't own." He spread his arms. "Which we aren't to blame for. We then asked the Swiss not to start investigations—who knows who's been asked to look away and how?"

"And?" Elodie asked.

"Well, the official consultations didn't get any further yet. However, I've got a personal contact with the Swiss—his relatives emigrated to Adelaide—with whom I discussed what we're expecting to find there. We agreed—if they're really training genetically upgraded warriors there, those would eat any Swiss agent for breakfast. Whereupon I proposed support by a special team to my contact, if he gets the formal obstacles cleared away."

"He can do that?"

"He can't. At least not without turning the truly big wheel. What he can do—he can ask us for an instructor team that will do an exercise with his people in the Alps and show them a few tricks. So much for the official reasoning. He can even make that decision on his own, as long as it doesn't eat up all his budget. I told him our people would like to spend their holidays in Switzerland, and wouldn't object against a little mountain exercise. Ain't it so, Tess?"

"My girls could profit from a change of scene. Always just training by swimming exercise is too limiting, isn't it?" She winked at us. "Okay, you've just finished a bouldering mission, but you surely unveiled improvement potential there."

"Of course," I sternly affirmed, and Elodie nodded.

"Formally it will be like this," Tess continued to explain. "The Swiss will get us in. Whoever blocks the area off surely has a walk-over with tourists, but they can't as easily brush off a unit of mountain infantry, not even if those appear together with an expanded platoon of foreign police consultants. Those are us, and that's another such exceptional case. The Swiss are neutral, and tolerating the presence of armed foreign forces could endanger their status. There are only two exceptions, and those are UN units, and Dragon territory citizens. The former, because they're protecting the entire planet including Switzerland and thus must know each terrain, and the latter because they're neutral, too."

"I understand." I glanced back and forth between Kenneth and Tess. "We're in this sense neutral?"

Kenneth nodded. "Yes, and thus you're enjoying the same freedom of travel without visa requirements as Jo and Arko themselves."

"Good — and in which way do we belong to the UN?"

"Not at all." The Australian's eyes flashed. "You'll be accompanied by an armor suit platoon, by Rashid's explicit request. For one, that gives your trip additional legitimation, and for two — his daughter Fatima shall get acquainted with Switzerland, too."

CHAPTER FIFTY-FOUR

Nothing could have underlined our mission's dangerousness better than the escort by thirty-six disguisable armor suits. I didn't buy into Kenneth's reasoning. The suits were doubtlessly meant to protect the Swiss once the going got tough.

Tess decided we'd be on our way without delay — should anything have seeped through, the opponent shouldn't have any extra time for preparations. Accordingly, the order went out to the armor suit commandant to deploy her unit at once.

So we mounted Zoé's Tigershark, collected the other Mambas during a stopover in Gladstone, and went on our way to Europe at Mach Four. Tess had a little time for a briefing during our journey. She stood in the central aisle, leaned against the cockpit door, and started repeating for the others what Arko, Elodie, Sabine, and I already knew.

Then she went on, "It will mainly be our job to explore the facility and deal with resistance. The Swiss will only take us into the blocked zone, and woe betide anyone trying to stop them. At this time, we're still holding back — we've been provided with Swiss uniforms without unit or rank insignia so that we won't stand out. The armor suits will follow us in camouflage. The opposition doesn't need to know about them either. Once we're close to the target, we'll take off the uniforms and rely on our protective suits alone. Once it's getting dark, we'll go in and have a look around."

"What's our mission objective?" Yvette asked. "Pure reconnaissance or termination?"

Tess briefly glanced at Arko. "We don't know what we'll meet there. A nest of determined criminals would have to be taken out before they could start the assault on Velvet Island. If we find youngsters who haven't been offered an alternative by anyone . . ."

Yes, we all knew that situation only too well.

"There will be staff," Kim argued. "For housekeeping, but also instructors and perhaps physicians, people responsible for the modifications."

"Anything else would be too easy," Lucy said. "You could simply blow up that place."

"Tsk," her partner Laura uttered. "Without asking the Dragonlings whether they'd prefer to work for Jo?"

"That's the other side of the problem," Tess agreed. "These people could be valuable support in our fight against the Jellies—if they want to. We must not gamble that away, even if it makes the mission more delicate for us."

Yvette nodded. "Fine. We sneak up there and have a look around, find out how many people we have to deal with, and if they invite us for tea, we'll make them an offer. How do we get ourselves synchronized if it goes another way?"

"If the situation topples, we must act fast," I stated. "We must not give these people time to get organized, otherwise we have no chance—that's the difficulty. It's not about an even duel. We're potentially the inferior ones, and if we're also short-handed, we have to use the moment of surprise."

"That sounds rather like termination again," Yvette said.

"I know. It won't be easy."

Tess raised both hands. "Slowly. What you say is true, Monique. If the opposition opts for battle, we must strike fast, with surprise, and hard. There's no room for experiments about effective narcotics or chains. To make the surprise work, we must remain unspotted until the last moment. Or, more precisely, as many of us as possible must remain unspotted. Sabine?"

"Just me," I said, before Tess's partner could reply. "I'm the only one of us with personal close combat experience. I have the best chance of surviving the next few seconds when it starts."

Tess wanted to argue, but she let me finish first.

"And because Lucy and Laura know how to shoot such a Dragonling if he doesn't want to stand still, they'd be the first choice to cover me."

Elodie gave me a surprised look.

I placed one hand on her arm. "I'm just stating the facts. I'd like to have you near me, but our planning hasn't got that far yet."

"Wait," Tess protested.

Now Arko chimed in. "Monique's assessment is logical. Her odds of survival are better, and against a single opponent quite good. Should it be possible to meet one Dragonling alone, or at least at some distance from the others, her assignment would be favorable."

Tess made a sour face, probably due to his interfering with her command. That had to be the price for taking him along.

I wasn't entirely sure if I should be grateful for his support or if he just had signed my death warrant, but I knew I couldn't forgive myself for mourning one of my teammates when I'd had a chance in the same situation.

Yes, I had a damn chance!

Our leader looked at me and frowned. "You really think you can tough that out?"

I nodded. "I can judge what to expect. I can judge these Dragonlings, and yes, I believe I can dodge their first strike. They won't take me by surprise — just the opposite, they'll be very surprised when I dodge, and then I'll have a fair chance to score myself. What happens thereafter . . ."

"Then we'll have to do it like this." She hesitated, opened

her mouth, closed it, looked away. Finally, she straightened herself. "Okay. Let's have a look at how we can support Monique effectively. The Swiss sent us an aerial of the area and an older construction plan for the farmstead. You can immediately see that the farmstead's been expanded by another building. Sabine and I incorporated the expansion from the aerial into the construction plan, and we will now memorize the building and examine for weaknesses. Moreover, I want you to know by heart each rock and each bush that could give us cover, and any obstacle that could impede our advance. Once we get the baseline straight, we'll talk about the approach in detail."

CHAPTER FIFTY-FIVE

Whoever had been responsible for coordination had done an extraordinarily good job—the two Tigersharks with the armor suits arrived virtually at the same time as ours over the little army airfield and flanked us. We approached touch-down in this formation.

Tess cleared her throat. "Gals, you've seen it. That's an ob-ligation. I have no doubt the suits will line up in perfect for-mation. Will we show them we can do the same?"

Of course we would—with our very personal flavor.

Once the plane had reached its final parking position and Zoé had extinguished the seat belt signs, Arko opened the door for us.

Like pearls on a string we easily jumped down to the air-field one by one, formed pairs, and swiftly followed our com-mand team.

While the armor suits marched up smartly and precisely, we floated into our positions in perfect choreography, as un-obtrusively as if we hadn't arrived yet. But when the last suits had reached their platoon's end and stood to attention, we Mambas faced them in six perfectly aligned rows of two—and exactly parallel to their formation.

This was another thing we'd had to learn—the formal drill was sometimes the best support for our self-control, if the drugs hadn't been balanced out well.

Focus on the formation and don't think of freaking out — that way you'll survive. You don't forget such a thing.

The suit leaders stood opposite Tess and Sabine, their faces

146

hidden behind golden masks.

Arko walked through our formation's center toward the Swiss. Only from the corner of my eyes, without turning my head, could I follow his way. Together with the brief glance I had been able to risk upon exiting the plane, I got a first impression. According to that, the Swiss were clearly outnumbered with their twenty-four soldiers and two officers.

"What are the *girls* doing here?" I heard one of the soldiers whisper with poor discipline and even less respect in a very accented German—ah, no, Swiss German.

"Welcome to Switzerland," the older of the two officers addressed Arko almost at the same time, while the younger one gave his men a stern glare. *"Protector* Ackrotzibähr? I am Major Hürtli of the Special Operations Command. This is Lieutenant Enzenberger of the Army Reconnaissance Battalion Ten."

"Please just call me Protector Arko." Our Dragon man spoke accent-free High German—in my ears a funny contrast to the Swiss' intonation. "The Dragon name is not made for human throats."

Arko pointed at the armor suits. "The Eleven-Eleven. First regiment, first battalion, first company, first platoon of the United Nations Armored Infantry, under command of Mrs. Brigadier General Fatima bint Rashid and her tandem partner and deputy Colonel Moses Perez. This unit will take care of the mission cover."

"The cover?" the major asked.

"The *Legata Aurea* sends her regards. According to the mission's importance, she asked the Secretary for Interstellar Defence to provide the Armored Infantry's elite platoon for our hosts' protection. The actual mission will be performed by her special unit for covert operations, the *Mambas.*" He pointed at us.

"I had understood that it's quite within the bounds of

possibility there'll be an engagement?" Major Hürtli aimed a doubtful glance in our direction.

"Exactly. Major, this is the special unit that prevented an American Marine Corps command from taking over Velvet Island. Each of these women has proven to be able to defeat an armor suit."

Oh, that made my day! Just as the major's next question did.

"So this is the unit the most recent Knights of the Order were recruited from?"

"And the last Squire. Right. Knight Zoé is our pilot."

The major squared his shoulders. "Protector Arko, the Legata Aurea and you must know significantly more about the upcoming mission than what's been contained in my briefing. Can you tell me and my men more?"

"We can, but I would propose a less public place for that."

"Oh, naturally. Please follow me. We've cleared one of the helicopter hangars. Lieutenant?"

The lieutenant nodded at one of the soldiers, probably the highest-ranking noncommissioned officer. The noncom dismissed the soldiers, and their formation dissolved.

Arko only gave Tess and one of the golden statues — with three stripes over the well-formed chest — a brief glance. Tess again just turned around and followed the major, while the suit bearer flicked her thumb, let her visor slide open, and then marched toward the hangar followed by her unit.

I focused on the soldier I had recognized as the source of the initial remark, and walked his way. He soon noticed me and waited for me to reach him. To my surprise, he reached out a hand.

"I'm Konrad," he said.

"Monique." I took his hand and shook it briefly and firmly.

He nodded. "You've got a firm grip. I'm sorry for the remark before. We were told almost nothing, sent here all of a sudden, and then—well, I felt somewhat run over and took my anger out to you. Nothing personal."

"No problem. And about information—we're getting to that."

CHAPTER FIFTY-SIX

For a few minutes I had thought that Arko's introduction had adjusted the image of us in the Swiss' heads for the better. Then Konrad, still walking at my side, asked, "At the next opportunity you might tell me how you enchanted the Marines. You didn't have to drop much, did you?"

I didn't honor him with an answer. *The first impression counts,* the saying went, and fixing it needed time. Time was what we didn't have, so why should I bother?

We had reached the hangar anyway. Our hosts had provided six rows of twelve chairs each facing an electronic wall panel and a small speaker's desk. Tess waved me close and walked up to the desk together with Arko and the two Swiss officers.

Fatima and Moses followed us a moment later while their teams were filling up the rows from the rear. That left four free chairs until Zoé arrived. The Swiss at the door tried to deny her entry — until he saw her order brooch. He let her pass with a smart salute and then closed the gate.

Tess didn't wait for anyone to give her the floor.

"From this moment on there's a significant chance that someone will report the news of our arrival to our mission target. Time is working against us, so we will brief you about the background now and go into the planning details right after. Monique, please report about your fight."

Major Hürtli seemed to be about to say something, but when Arko glanced at him, he remained silent.

I stepped to the microphone and gazed across the waiting

soldiers' faces. "My partner and I were about to lead the three targets freed in the course of our mission out of the building. Other mission participants had involved the defenders in a firefight. Then there was the encounter."

Only the facts, I told myself, less to the Swiss' advantage but for our critical Dragon man whom I didn't want to give reason to ask questions. After all, I wasn't telling the story for the first time. I knew which details mattered.

"Thank you, Monique," Tess said afterward and turned to the major. "Do you have questions?"

"A highly interesting description." The major scrutinized me. "Only perhaps a bit embellished in the details regarding the course of the fight?"

Tess smirked and nodded at me. We had expected my story to be hard to believe — some people had to see first what a Mamba could do, and we usually didn't advertise it. These people here had to know what to expect if they met a Drag-onling.

I made two steps forward and looked at three of the soldiers in turn. "Attack me."

The three glanced at each other, grinned, and slowly rose. I gave them time enough to focus their attention on me. Then I called up my booster.

One of our most useful abilities was not to give ourselves away by tensing muscles, a sideward glance, or taking a deep breath. The only advance warning my first opponent got was my jump at him from standing, and he was lying on the ground before he had a chance to react. This short time didn't help his neighbor — one moment later I had levered him off his legs, too.

Number three at least managed to raise his arms for defense, only it didn't help him any more than the others. My acceleration allowed me to get around any of his movements without effort. Next, he was lying on the ground.

Before the majority of spectators had even realized my fight had begun, I had returned to my starting position. Now they watched my opponents get back on their feet in awe.

"Did you see how I did it, or should I demonstrate it again, only slower?" I studied their movements — had they taken it as good sports, or should I expect a panicked reaction?

"Impressive." Had Major Hürtli had the same thoughts? In any case, he approached me. "I withdraw my objections. Your report obviously wasn't exaggerated, Mamba Monique. And I begin to understand why you've only envisaged a supporting role for us on this mission."

CHAPTER FIFTY-SEVEN

The unfamiliar uniform flapped around my body, and the protective vest pressed heavily on my breasts. Boots and beret bothered me comparably little.

Konrad examined me critically. "That's doesn't fit correctly. May I help?"

"Sure."

He plucked around in a few places, let me raise my arms, walked around me once, and then he nodded. "This must do. More can't be done without a tailor."

"It doesn't have to work for long. It only has to fit well enough not to embarrass you until we're in the target area."

"That'll be okay." He looked out of the gate, where the buses were already waiting for us. "Are you afraid?"

"Uh — what?"

"I'd be afraid. No, that's not quite true. I *am* afraid. If anything goes wrong and these guys start hunting us, we barely have any chance, do we?"

"You shouldn't even get close enough that they notice you. Just keep your heads down."

"Yeees — we shall *fight defensively,* such a nonsense. Either I see the enemy coming and aim for it before it gets me, or I dig in and thus don't fight."

"Well, a bit of both. Bullets are effective."

"We're lucky. But what about you — are you afraid?"

"No."

"No? Honestly?"

"Honestly." I looked into his eyes. "I've learned not to be

153

afraid."

"You can learn that?"

"Whoever is afraid will make mistakes. Whoever makes a mistake will die. The survivors learned not to be afraid. As easy as that."

"Will die? You mean there were accidents?"

"Oh, those happened, and executions."

"Executions?"

"With the garrote. Very instructive."

He made a face. "Who reports to such a unit? That's madness."

"The recruitment isn't voluntary."

"No? But—" He stared at me helplessly.

"We were trained by the Cartel, Konrad, and inferior material was *sorted out,* until only the very best remained. In the end, you got used to the danger."

"By the Cartel . . . but why?"

"As killers. We were trained to kill Johanna. She beat us to it—and offered us an alternative. I'm glad to have had this choice, and I'm proud of having made the right decision."

Konrad still stared at me. Then he stood to attention and saluted. This time, I felt he was honest.

I returned the salute.

We gazed at each other another moment. There was no need to say anything more. We both turned and walked to the buses.

CHAPTER FIFTY-EIGHT

The buses stopped in the middle of the narrow paved road. The driver let the door of our bus swing open, we exited, and lined up at its side along the mountain meadow's edge, two soldiers and a team of Mambas in turns. Our shadows tried to crawl under the buses. I knew the disguised armor suits were somewhere close to us, but I was too interested in the events before us to look for giveaways now.

Lieutenant Enzenberger and two of his soldiers were already walking up to a low white-painted wooden gate. A young man in decent leather pants and checkered shirt was leaning on it.

That man now pushed himself away and stood before the uniformed men. "What are you doing here?"

"We're on our way to the maneuver. Please step aside," the lieutenant said.

"Maneuver? That's not possible, this is a restricted area."

"So? I don't think you're authorized to give orders to the army. Our maneuver has been coordinated with the responsible authorities, and there's no information on restricted areas."

"This area is private."

"Firstly, this only applies partially, and secondly, it doesn't matter for this maneuver. The proprietors may of course claim eventual damages resulting from our maneuver. Now please step aside."

Tess whispered something to the soldier next to her and covertly pointed at the forest edge some way above the meadow. I followed her gesture and squinted. Yes, that could be a rifle barrel. Were these people ready to shoot ordinary mountain hikers? And if so, were they also ready to take up the army?

Sabine had, also covertly, already drawn her plasma pistol and unfolded the gunstock. Two hundred meters, I estimated. A difficult shot, but not impossible.

The addressed soldier passed the information on to the major, and the major sent him to his lieutenant.

"I may not let you pass," the young man there insisted.

The lieutenant shook his head, spotted the new arrival and turned to him. "Yes?"

The soldier stood next to his lieutenant, his back to the leather pants man, pointed at the forest edge, and made a sign.

Lieutenant Enzenberger nodded and made another manual sign before he addressed the young man again very loudly and clearly. "You must step aside, and you may complain to the responsible authorities. You may not impede a legitimate maneuver of the active forces if you don't want us to arrest you for military treason right away. The same applies to your supporter up there in the forest."

The young man's head twitched before he could make up his mind, but he had already betrayed himself. The barrel, hardly visible between the leaves, trained around toward the lieutenant—Sabine went on her knee, aimed, and shot in a single, fast move.

A cry of pain came from the forest. Lucy and Laura were already on their way, and a brief nod by the major sufficed to make two of his men follow.

The soldiers around us kept their assault rifles up and scanned the area. Elodie stayed put at my side just like the other Mambas.

The leather pants man looked around.

"Don't even think about it," Enzenberger advised him. "You're arrested."

"I didn't do anything!"

"The judge will look into that. Take him away."

That was what his soldiers then did. Not much later, the assigned soldiers pulled the injured sniper from the forest. Sabine had aimed well and only hit his arm — which in case of a plasma pistol nevertheless meant a permanent souvenir.

Major Hürtli nodded at Tess. "You were right. Something big is going on here. Who'd take on the Swiss army?"

"We must go. These people must know they can't stay once they're busted. If we still want to find someone . . ."

"I understand. Well, our usefulness has been short-lived, hasn't it?"

"I wouldn't say that . . ." Our leader paused because she had seen something.

Laura returned from the forest edge. "No radio."

"Astonishing," Tess commented. "So we can stick to Plan A for a while."

CHAPTER FIFTY-NINE

Konrad was panting heavily when we finally stopped short before the knoll. After the hour-long walk and the subsequent speedy climb across six-hundred meters altitude, he was supposed to show signs of exhaustion.

"It doesn't seem to bother you," he whispered at me.

"It was strenuous," I admitted. "I just don't show it."

Then I began to take off the protective vest, as the other Mambas did, too. The boots followed, then the cumbersome uniform, and finally the beret. Lastly I put on the holster and pulled a wide-cut red walking coat from the backpack.

"You're the *messenger?*" Konrad asked.

I nodded. *The messenger*, that was my code name, the code name for the person that would expose herself. We hadn't mentioned the role assignment in our final briefing for the Swiss.

Konrad's question encompassed more. From the Swiss' point of view, this role especially was a suicide mission. I had a different view, but this wasn't the moment to discuss it. "This is a beautiful night to die," I said.

Indeed our host country showed its best side — no clouds in the sky, the mountain peaks majestically rising before the stars' backdrop, pleasantly fresh temperatures — it could have been a wonderful vacation day, and it was a marvelous change from our home's ocean panorama.

The other Mambas assembled around Tess. The soldiers silently watched her place one hand on each woman's shoulder, nod at them, and release them to their mission duties. My teammates looked hot in their skintight black protective suits, and more than one Swiss quietly sighed when another two of them disappeared into the dark of dusk.

Elodie gave me a last glance back before following Sabine and Tess. I winked at her.

The Mambas had half an hour to reach their positions. The first teams had to reach the farthest points in the valley, then go wide around the farmstead. The last ones had an easier approach, but should be spotted even less.

As opposed to them, it was my task to be spotted. In exchange, I had plenty of time for my approach.

I gave Konrad a nod as goodbye and walked past the other resting soldiers up the path.

The last one I passed was Major Hürtli. He stepped aside and made a sad face. "Good luck, Mamba Monique."

"Thanks."

I left him standing with that and swiftly marched up the path, suppressing the brief urge to turn back and yell at them, "I'm not dead yet!"

Instead, I focused on my role of the lone mountain hiker who didn't want to climb down to the road after dark and was glad to find an obviously inhabited farmstead.

Our plan was based on the assumption that a lone woman openly approaching the farmstead wouldn't be shot without warning. If I only managed to get close enough to relay my message . . .

CHAPTER SIXTY

Only a few of the farmstead's windows were still illuminated, and even those were closed with robust blinds, so that the shine of light didn't reach far. So I stuck to my role and occasionally stumbled over a rock on the path, and started when finally a tall man in black leather appeared before me and shone at my face with a torch. I automatically turned my head to the side so as not to be blinded.

"Stop! Who are you, and what are you doing here?"

"Uh — one moment." With one hand on the left side of my chest, I took three deep breaths, the other hand shielded my eyes against his torch. "I'm Monique Arnaud. It got late, and I don't want to climb down into the valley now. Do you have a toilet?"

"Where do you come from?"

"I'm from Belgium. I don't know my way around the mountains at all."

He lowered his torch. "You shouldn't be here."

"No, agreed. But here I am now."

"This is a restricted area. No trespassing."

"I didn't see a sign, I'm sorry. Well, it's none of my business why this area is restricted, but is it helpful if I further stumble around in the dark?"

"You've seen too much already."

"Really? I haven't seen anything — it's dark."

He came closer and took the upper part of my left arm with a firm grip. "Stop mocking me."

"Ouch!" I protested, within my role, and tried to tear

myself free. "Hey, what did I do to you? Let me go!"

"Stop wriggling and come with me." He pushed me toward the entrance door, only recognizable by the narrow illuminated crack.

A well-lit, spacious breakfast kitchen and a group of six brawny giants of different ages were waiting for me behind the door. Their vintage was hard to tell. They were wearing uniform white tracksuits and looked similar, like siblings. Only their beards and hairdos differed.

Six Dragonlings together—I saw my odds for survival diminish rapidly. The guy still holding my arm didn't count in that regard.

"Who are you bringing us?" one of the supposedly older Dragonlings with a narrow moustache asked. That way, he identified himself as the alpha, the group leader.

"The little one calls herself Monique and claims to have lost her way."

"I didn't lose my way," I immediately protested. "It got late, and I didn't want to go down to the valley in the dark."

"So, you didn't lose your way?" the alpha asked. "What are you doing here, then?"

"I asked him for a toilet." I nodded toward my guard. "Moreover, I've got a message to relay."

"You've got a *message?*" The alpha raised his eyebrows. His mates were still showing poker faces. "For us? So you deliberately came here?"

"She didn't tell me about that!" my guard protested and squeezed my arm tighter again. This time, I simply ignored him.

"Shut up!" the alpha barked at him and then focused on me again. "What's your message?"

"You know about the Jelly's second wave." That was just a hope, but my counterpart didn't object. "Mankind needs any help. There's always a place for able men and women in the Legata Aurea's team. Johanna Meier offers you a job."

Upon the Legata's mention, his eyes flashed furiously, but now he asked, "She offers *us* a job?"

He gazed at his people, who gazed at him, and then at me again.

"And for that she sends one *girl?*"

I shrugged with my free arm's shoulder. "Where's the problem? I'm sufficiently qualified to relay such a message. More isn't required by Dragon logic."

"What do you know about Dragon logic?"

Another shrug. "As much as I need to. Everyone is assigned where his abilities are most useful. That may be at a spaceship's wheel, in exploration of a distant planet, or as messenger."

Two of the younger Dragonlings perked up their ears upon this statement. Had I placed the right bait?

"Or for the exploration of a secret research center," the alpha continued my enumeration and squinted. "What exactly is your mission here?"

My part of this mission was accomplished, the message relayed, and the situation was about to topple. I saw the alpha tensing his muscles but still holding back.

How long did a Dragonling need to heat up his booster?

CHAPTER SIXTY-ONE

It was obvious that the alpha wasn't heating up to shake hands with me, and I wasn't eager to learn in detail what else he was up to.

Unlike he did, I didn't need a longer phase to heat up, and unlike he did, I didn't give myself away by tensing my muscles.

In a single instant, I went to speed, spun the guard at my arm around, tossed him into the alpha's way, and broke through the door behind me with a dive and follow-up roll. Outside I doubled to the side, tore the telltale bright coat off — the prepared seams gave up as planned — and drew my pistols, right in time to serve the Dragonling coming after me with two sun-hot plasma balls.

The surprise worked, the shots fully scored. I didn't have to see more — instead, I turned around and ran off at top speed.

According to the noises following me, I was being chased by at least two more Dragonlings — and those were faster than me!

Obviously they had no trouble recognizing me despite my black suit. Conversely, Elodie and Sabine had no trouble recognizing my pursuers in their white suits and so opened fire with appropriate lead.

The sound of running feet behind me fell mute, so I stopped and looked back. One of the Dragonlings — or what was left of him — was lying motionless in the grass, and the other was attacking Sabine.

She didn't get time for another shot, she could barely dodge, then Tess moved in and deflected his next smash to the side. Her painful cry stopped when the Dragonling's swinging arm hit her chest and tossed her away like an annoying fly. She just lay there, unmoving.

Meanwhile Sabine had gotten back on her feet, so that she could dodge the next attack *fast*. But the Dragonling followed up and grazed her again.

This was a different caliber from my opponent in the mountain fortress—strong enough to stand his ground against several experienced Mambas. Nevertheless I attacked him now, scissored his legs away and pushed him to the ground.

Before he could overcome the surprise, I pulled my legs out of his reach and jumped up again. Sabine eluded his direct access, too, while the Dragonling catapulted himself up like a jumping bean. A heatwave threatened to steal our breath, and I guessed our opponent had switched a notch higher. How should we defeat him now?

Two plasma rounds added more energy to the already hot body—Elodie had scored!

His right arm was scorched black. The second shot had only grazed his rump, and now he was storming at us again.

Sabine dashed to the side, and I jumped into his rampage, between his legs, and levered him over me.

He instantly reacted and closed his thighs around my head. Had he squeezed now, my head would simply have burst.

We came down on our backs heavily, and his clamp weakened a little—but not enough to set me free.

But he had missed a little detail—as long as he held me, I had a safe target, and I had hoped for that. Thus I was already holding my plasma pistols in my hands, so I pressed them into the hollows of his knees, and pulled the triggers.

Both knees exploded, boiling flesh sprayed across my

protective suit, and the pressure at my head vanished when the impact shock ran up his leg muscles.

I rolled to the side and pulled one gun over my head. The next shot hit his kidney area.

CHAPTER SIXTY-TWO

A dark silhouette leaned over me.
"How do you feel?" my partner whispered.

"Like a fried chicken." Our suits deflected heat, too, but I had to get by with a few scalded spots. "I'm combat-ready."

She held out a hand, and I let her pull me up. Worried, I peeked into the dark.

"How's Tess doing?"

Elodie shrugged and glanced over there. Another dark shape was kneeling over the body on the ground. Now Sabine rose and gave us a thumbs-up, then she helped Tess get up.

Tess watched the farmstead. We heard the hiss of plasma weapons from there, crashing wood, the crackling of flames, single calls or cries. There, more Dragonlings were waiting for us, but meanwhile, our teammates were involved in fighting there, too. "Come," she said.

The four of us hurried toward the building that was burning in several places. Tess turned right and pointed left, so Elodie and I left those two and headed for the building's left side, where I just had departed from.

"Not another such stunt, please," Elodie demanded. "My heart almost stopped."

"Believe me, it wasn't fun for me either. I felt like I was in a vise — but it worked."

"Yes."

Moreover, I'd soon know how much his hot thighs had fried my ears, not to mention my own plasma shots' side effects. However, we weren't through with the fire subject yet.

Elodie pointed at the door frame to the breakfast kitchen. I nodded and sneaked up there, both pistols ready. She followed me at a close distance.

Quick steps sounded from inside, then three older women came running out. They ignored us, so we ignored them, too — particularly as someone inside now uttered a terrible, four-voiced roar.

My misjudgment became apparent when the four noise sources separated, but we had no time to discuss this phenomenon, as one of them came toward us, and *fast*.

We had just managed to press ourselves to the outer wall next to the door when a tall white shape jumped outside, rolled off, turned around, spotted us, and instantly came for us.

I served two shots and dashed sideways-forward, away from Elodie. The Dragonling howled, hit, brushed Elodie away with a single move of his arm, crashed into the wall, and made the entire building tremble. My companion flew through the air, tumbled a few times upon landing and then lay on the ground, apparently lifeless.

I managed to get back up on my feet about the same time as the Dragonling, shot again and ran toward the building's corner — to find cover and lure him away from Elodie.

At least the plan's second part worked, but before I could reach the corner, I already had to dodge my raging pursuer.

His strike only grazed my right arm. *Ouch!* The plasma pistol flew away — my stunned fingers couldn't hold the weapon.

Thus he had successfully moved himself between myself and the house and was forcing me into the open field — that wasn't good at all. His body heat radiated for meters and drove the sweat out of my pores, and he was already striking at me again. Only a swift jump let me dodge, but I didn't manage to gain distance.

He tried to throw himself at me, and again I only barely escaped. That wouldn't go well for long! He was faster than me, and a single hit could take me out—in turn, I had no chance on him.

Or did I? I hadn't really tried yet!

I dived under his clasping grip, jumped forward to escape the following scythe strike, doubled over to the side and re-sisted the temptation to roll forward—once I was on the ground, I was doomed.

That guy had to have a weak spot, and I wouldn't need to try kicking his balls. Ouch—dodged too tightly, and he'd al-most managed to grab my dull right arm.

Why didn't his injuries impede him? A grazing hit at the arm, okay, but that severe burn across his chest . . . hey! that was my toehold!

I just had to get close. Only one try, once again, and this time there was no Elodie to get me out in case I failed.

Right—this time I went into his attack fully, only briefly dodged to escape his fist, raised my mostly useless right arm toward his eyes as a feint—his head jerked back—and drove my left's fingers into his boiling-hot chest, through between his ribs—oh, that burned! Into his lung, then through his heart.

My fingers seemed to burn up, even though my glove's ro-bust nano fabric prevented worse. But my opponent arched, stumbled, pulsed surges of hot blood over me, collapsed, pulled me down with him, and died.

My view turned black.

CHAPTER SIXTY-THREE

*E*lodie!
There was a heavy pressure on the chest, making my breathing hard, burning pain all over my body, weakness, some nausea. Where was I, where was my partner?

I opened my eyes and saw blackness . . . with blurred specks of light. Stars?

Heat and loud crackling in the immediate vicinity made it appear advisable to move. But there still was this weight that also pressed my arms to my body.

I pushed the burden up with a power boost, away from me, and registered it was a lifeless body, from which a warm stream ran across my arms—the dead Dragonling.

I wasn't Siegfried, and he wasn't Fafnir, so this bath in his blood wouldn't help me. Relieved from his corpse's burden, I could at least stand up now.

Ouch.

I hobbled the first steps until the pain in my legs turned into a dull burning feeling. At least nothing was broken. I covered the remaining short distance to my partner a bit faster.

She was lying on her back, motionless, the left arm impossibly twisted. I knelt at her side and felt for her pulse at her throat. Weak, but present. Breath? My hand over her nose sensed nothing, but then she moved her head, opened her eyes, raised her right arm and pushed my hand away.

"Can you manage?"

"Arm . . ."

"Looks broken."

Elodie took several deep breaths, then she tried to move the arm and cried out.

She focused on me. "Dislocated. Help me."

"Okay." That would hurt, but it was always better than leaving the arm dislocated. I put one foot against her ribs close to the armpit, took her wrist, and then pulled her arm and pushed it sideways with my foot. Clack!

"How's it going?"

"Much better." She gave a tired smile. "Get going."

She didn't have to tell me twice. Our mates were fighting at the other side! But it would've been out of the question to let my partner suffocate while unconscious.

My first impression was — it wouldn't work. We were losing.

Three almost unhurt Dragonlings were fighting against five Mambas in the farmstead's rear — Tess tried to support Yvette, Gwen and Sabine fought another Dragonling, Tia was fighting alone. I didn't see Lucy and Laura. I had passed Kim at the building corner, Justine was lying motionless under the Dragonling who fought Tia, and Avril was leaning on the wall with her back, not far away from a window frame burning brightly.

The individual fights went too fast to place a well-aimed shot. Tia needed help most urgently, but Tess and Yvette were closest to me.

The Dragonling was dealing out and roaring. Tess flew away, Yvette ducked — then a kick hit her. Yvette moaned and remained down. Almost at the same time I saw Sabine and Tia going down further behind.

I couldn't help them all — I only had one pistol and currently two possible targets. So I placed one shot at the Dragonling who was about to finish Tia off, and tried a foot lever with the guy right before me.

But I had given up my moment of surprise with the shot, and with my attempted attack I had also brought myself deep into his reach. Stupid mistake—deadly mistake! His next strike would shatter me, and I couldn't get away.

CHAPTER SIXTY-FOUR

The earth seemed to tremble, my ears buzzed, my bones were vibrating, so loud was the angry, challenging roar that seemed to come from everywhere.

My opponent simply let me lie and dashed away.

I watched him leave.

His target was a snake-like, winged creature that rose meters-high above the Dragonling who just before had threatened Tia. A talon-armed foot pressed the formerly invincible-looking opponent to the ground.

The last Dragonling had simply ignored Gwen and stormed at the Dragon, as if to attack him from behind.

One lash with the tail—he flew across the air for meters, dropped to the ground.

My Dragonling wrapped his arms around the Dragon's neck, pressed hard. One wing came down, the wing thorn barely caressed the attacker, but the man twitched, relaxed, and dropped down, reared up once, then he no longer moved.

"Situation?" Arko thundered.

"Lucy and Laura are missing," I uttered.

"Inside the house," Avril's quiet voice added from behind me. Only now did I notice that all sounds except for the crackling fire had fallen silent.

This gigantic Dragon wouldn't fit in there . . . but yes! The next moment, Arko jumped toward the door, moved his head inside, the snake body followed, even the folded wings moved through the frame until only the tail tip poked out, and everywhere around the wood was burning!

I hurried to pull Avril away from the danger zone.

"Thank you," she wheezed.

Then the house cracked and crunched, and Arko broke through the burning roof with spread-out wings, jumped outside, came down on his hind legs, and placed two lifeless shapes down on the grass very carefully.

"Call Zoé. These two must get into the tank."

That surely applied not just to these two. My radio was probably burned, though, as it was as quiet as a mouse.

Avril assumed this task.

Now I saw golden figures coming from several directions, spread across the area, group around injured Mambas or dead and living inhabitants. The Swiss' darker silhouettes followed somewhat later.

"How are you?" I asked Avril.

"I can't feel my legs anymore." She looked up at me with a worried face. "I can't feel anything down there."

"Hush. That's no problem for our healing nanos."

By and by, more Mambas assembled around us—Elodie with Kim, Gwen, Tess, Sabine, Yvette. Tia brought Justine with her.

A pair of armor suits approached the Dragon. Both saluted, one talked. "Protector, one of our teams picked up two of these Dragonlings. They surrendered without resistance and asked for admittance. One said they'd like to accept the offer. Can you make something of that?"

"Of course." After all, Arko had designed the message that I had relayed. "Please bring them to me."

"Yes, *Protector*."

CHAPTER SIXTY-FIVE

One after the other, we all had to go into the tank, with more or less severe burns, broken bones, cuts, lacerations, and contusions. But we hadn't lost anyone!

The two young Dragonlings who had opted for the right side would doubtlessly become a worthy reinforcement for our expedition team—once you became acquainted with them, they were both quite amiable.

Aside from these men, we had freed eight women. The older Dragonlings had abused some of these women as birthing machines, and so one of them was advanced in pregnancy. She'd soon deliver another Dragonling. Even if that boy was the product of rape, Johanna might be able to convince the woman not to blame the child. Perhaps she wouldn't even regard it as a monster one day.

Doubtlessly, Nanette's and Jo's tender care would do the women good, but initially they were accommodated in a guaranteed male-free environment on the mainland and attended by psychologists there.

The Dragonlings provided us with further intel on the program, as far as they knew about it. The first Dragonlings had been sired by a transformed Dragon in the nineties of the previous century—that had to be one of the conspirators of the venture which Zoe Lionheart had ended with the *Nemrut Battle.*

The program had thereafter been continued in different places. The Dragonling genes were conveniently dominant, so that the union of a Dragonling and any woman always created another Dragonling — our new arrivals couldn't tell us how that had been achieved, though. They hadn't been introduced to this secret yet, and the men who had known were dead. They hadn't been able to resist Arko's terrible *Wyvern* poison.

Jo, like Arko before, also *remembered* that the Lionheart had met one of these early Dragonlings — first in Cologne, then again in Cairo. The Lionheart had had a hard time defeating this opponent. We could therefore be very proud to have disposed of five of them without Arko's help!

Only — I felt no pride. These men could have helped us if they hadn't been so brick-headed. They could have played a better role than that of an elite criminal gang.

Intelligence seemingly hadn't mattered in their genetical design, at least aside from the two of them who had chosen smartly. Well, their brains didn't matter that much. We had smart brains by the score, so two guys for muscle jobs were very welcome, most of all with such good looks and such long cocks.

If I could pick my reward . . .

To be continued . . .

You may also enjoy the following from eXtasy Books Inc:

Loonie
Valerie J. Long

Excerpt

I must be a total lunatic. That thought suddenly shot through my mind, and I paused in my movement. My nude body clung tight to the building's mirror-like face. With nothing more than the suckers at my finger and toe tips, I stuck like a gecko almost three hundred meters above the ground on the outside wall of the Frostdragon corporate skyscraper. I must be a total lunatic. However, of course my climb made sense.

The four-hundred-and-seventy-six-meters high building was practically impenetrable for a burglar. The main and rear entrances were well guarded, just as the accesses to staircases and elevator shafts were. The roof held a landing pad for helicopters or Tigershark planes with perfect surveillance. In between, the building was wrapped in panes of diamond-hardened armor glass, almost without grooves, only interrupted by finger-sized openings for the antennas of metal and motion detectors. Glass cutters were useless—there was no way through! But far above, at four hundred thirty-eight meters, there was a maintenance access for the illuminated company name. If you could get out there, you could get in there, too. At least, I assumed so—I'd have to have a look once I arrived there.

Metallic equipment was out of the question, as such would make all bells ring. The motion detectors—yes, I could deceive them, at least until now. As with other, rather ground-bound missions, their sensitivity had been toned down so that no ordinary bird would raise an alarm. Moreover, the surveillance didn't reach the windows, according to the vendor's specifications. I only had to stay close to the wall.

The suckers on finger and toe tips had been morphed forward. With some preparation, that worked just like more robust skin, against scratches and such. I could camouflage my skin and my stubbly hairdo like a chameleon. Here, no pale blot stuck to the façade—I was as dark as the unlit room next to my belly. At my fingers and toes, I felt the air conditioner's fine vibrations. All that still appeared like a dream to me, but I didn't want to pinch myself now. The nano machines that I had injected myself with were making all this possible. I could comprehend it in my mind, but, to my feelings, it was still strange. Better senses had developed as subtly as my athletic skills—faster, stronger, more precise. Was a three-meter jump from standing to the second floor normal? For me, it was. Whatever could make me better was welcome. I took what I could get and then made the best of it. Good wasn't good enough for me. So I asked myself—which other special abilities could my nanos create for me? I had had to take so often, I desired more resistance. I need more power!

—Performance enhancement program is not completed yet.—

Oops. Hello, Ghost.

Almost everything worked intuitively. To me, it seemed awkward to talk to myself. Moreover, it was dangerous. What if I accidentally talked to myself aloud? And why should I? I knew what I had to know about myself, and I could control myself, like, for example, my camouflage. This nano integration was ingenious even if I didn't walk around in my head.

Technically, I was lunatic—that is, deviating from the norm, different than other people. At the same time, thanks to my nanos, my mind was clearer than ever before. So why did I hang from a skyscraper three hundred meters above the ground? Because I was loony enough to try.

Three of four extremities—fifteen suckers—should have contact simultaneously to carry my low body weight, otherwise I'd be going down! That, too, limited the amount of equipment I could carry around. I had to save on clothes, so instead my skin showed the right camouflage coloring. Hey— I had never before burgled nude! Wasn't that loony?

Too much dust on the glass or even soap would have been the end of my climb—bye, Jo! Rain would be the last thing I needed now, but that's what weather forecasts were for. I could have guessed that it would be rather windy up here and thus chilly—now I simply had to suffer the temperatures. I shouldn't even tremble!

Okay, one third of the distance still lay ahead of me, so I should tackle that remainder now. It was the right foot's turn. Cautiously, I detached the five toes from the window and applied them ten centimeters higher again. A quick test proved to me that they had suction, so I moved my body some way up. Next was the left hand. And so on.

Move by move, I approached the green lit letters. Move by move, I adapted my body color to the stray light. Where exactly would I find access now?

A narrow grid catwalk ran between the letters and the wall. Great! Not only that I'd finally find a safe hold there, this catwalk wouldn't be covered by motion sensors. After the hours-long climb, I looked forward to a short break—even if it only was for my nerves, which hadn't found a moment's rest. I shouldn't rush now, though—the last moves had to come patiently, so that I wouldn't lose my grip on the last centimeters.

It cost me more self control than power to reach the cat-walk. After more than two hours of climbing, I was simply worn out. I could grant myself a few minutes there, control pulse and blood pressure, take a deep breath, and relax my muscles. I soothed my bad conscience by telling myself I'd wait and see whether my presence would trigger any reaction, and moreover, I needed calm hands for the next step.

With the climbing alone, I wasn't done yet. I wanted to get inside the building, to the executive floor and into one of the offices there. In order to get there, I first had to deal with the door, probably locked from inside, that led to my grid cat-walk.

This proved easy. As it should be primarily impossible to reach, with the catwalk undetected from outside, sloppiness had snuck in — nobody had cared to lock the door. Thus the door — which could never remain open due to the strong wind at this height — could simply be pulled open at its lever. Next I stood in the spacious airlock chamber. Right next to the door I could read advice in multiple languages to always keep the outside door shut and never open it together with the inside door, so that the rush of air wouldn't cause havoc inside the building.

Most importantly, I wasn't interested in a rush of air stirring up the guards, so I nicely closed the outside door before I very gently pulled at the inside door. Gently, so that the pressure equalization inside the chamber wouldn't trigger any plop or crack sounds inside the building. Then I was inside, and nobody knew of my presence.

In order to keep it that way, I adapted my skin color to the dull-pale wall color. I knew roughly how many surveillance cameras had to be installed inside the building overall, because I had procured the respective vendor data before — only one of the numerous exploration missions I had performed in preparation of this prowl. From the number, I could easily tell that not only emergency staircases and elevator access were secured. However, I hadn't been able to find precise installation plans for all floors—there was a general instruction for just these staircases and elevators and a few detailed sketches for the reception area and the executive floor. If one of the cameras was aimed at this door, my mission would fail here and now.

No, tonight fortune favored the bold. Nobody could observe the maintenance door opening and closing. Despite my invisibility, I wouldn't have been able to do anything about it.

I still faced a similar problem, as I'd have to cover another twelve floors to reach the executive floor. I could use the camera-guarded elevator or a well-secured emergency staircase—or had I rather follow the cliché and use the tight, always silver-colored, rectangular, and astonishingly well-lit air condition duct?

Neither of these options appealed to me. I instead searched access to the maintenance shaft for the in-house network, squeezed through the maintenance flap and began the strenuous climb between the glass fiber cables. If I wasn't susceptible to acrophobia outside, now my disposition toward claustrophobia was put to the test. Only someone of my stature would fit inside here at all, and only someone with a nano-technically adapted skin could wind his or her way between the cables and cable bridges without cutting him or herself a few dozen times. Of course, my stamina was also tested another time, even if I only had to cover about thirty meters.

Frostdragon's executive floor indeed seemed to be deserted this night. This wasn't typical for a large international corporation, but there were nights like these, when the entire board of directors, including their respective staffs, had to attend an external event. These events weren't exactly broadcasted to the public, but those who could read the signs could find out something. The best sources were the host's preparations—Frostdragon Australia had perked itself up, so they expected important visitors.

The fireproof flap to the cable duct was diligently closed

again. Before I stepped from the small service room into the hallway, I checked the surroundings with a little mirror — one of the few devices I had brought, after all there wasn't much room in my cheek pouch. It wasn't just the afore-mentioned weight problem. To maintain my camouflage I also had to wear any equipment inside my body.

I'd only regard this floor as empty once I'd checked that personally. The little mirror with the folding grip not only told me that the hallway was empty, but also that no camera lens was observing the door, before I pushed it farther open and stepped outside.

My skin was already adjusting to the high-class wooden tiling's patterns that were predominant on this floor. First, I cast a brief worried glance down — how much did the carpet give in under my bare feet? All my camouflage wouldn't help if I gave myself away there.

No, I didn't give myself away. The decorator hadn't opted for fluffy luxury, but for practical, coffee-proof, antistatic, difficult-to-ignite carpeting with pepper-and-salt pattern, on which I could sneak along marvelously quietly.

I'd have most liked to keep my track short and pick the office right behind the next door. But the offices on this side faced the city and thus also were visible from there — I needed an office where the computer screen would shine on an uninhabited area, and that could only be found on the ocean side. For this purpose, I had to round the floor once, across the elevators and the emergency staircase door, and across the reception for the administrative office of the board and the guard located there, too.

The presence of a guard didn't surprise me. First, no responsible head of security would rely on electronic systems alone that could fail or be cheated. Second, surveillance cameras couldn't act against intruders like me. Until an express elevator from the ground could arrive here, precious seconds would have passed.

Moreover, the man wore a Frostdragon armor suit made

from nano material. This way, he could camouflage himself almost as well as I could, was protected against light firearms, blades and fire, and his visor gave him infrared view, motion detection and similar gimmicks. For guard service, there was no need for the backpack with micro fusion reactor and heavy linear cannons — after all, we weren't at war — instead he wore an ordinary pistol in a holster made of nano material at his hip. This way, it would be camouflaged, too, as long as he didn't draw the weapon.

However, he wasn't camouflaged, didn't wear his hood and visor, but sat in a swivel chair behind the reception counter, bored, browsed a men's magazine, and sipped a coffee. Understandable — probably nobody had been able to intrude to this point since the building's first time use, and on a day where no persons were present to be protected — and nobody checked him — you could go easy, couldn't you?

The easy attitude couldn't deceive me. This man could become dangerous to me. He was wide awake and did his job, looked up each time he turned a page to check his surroundings. One telltale noise would put him on my heels.

My best option was to crawl along the bottom of the counter. There, he couldn't see me even if my camouflage wasn't entirely perfect, and if I was cautious and breathed lightly, he wouldn't hear me either. Moreover, the cameras couldn't spot me there.

I only had to reach the counter first. I'd have preferred to hurry the few steps across once he turned the page and focused on the next. But that was no option — the surge of air could give me away. No, I had to place one step after the other, keep my camouflage adapted and freeze my moves when he looked up. Like he did now.

About the Author

I am Valerie J. Long, born in 1963. I live and work in Germany as an IT project manager. I like role playing games, and I like putting my ideas on paper. I like all kinds of Science Fiction and Fantasy, I like music, and I like making you bite your nails off.

www.ingramcontent.com/pod-product-compliance
Lightning Source LLC
Chambersburg PA
CBHW060815120626
46557CB00001B/227